F[illegible]

A CO[illegible]

Cowboy Dreamin' 3

Sandy Sullivan

Erotic Romance

Secret Cravings Publishing
www.secretcravingspublishing.com

A Secret Cravings Publishing Book

Erotic Romance

For the Love of a Cowboy

Print ISBN: 978-1-63105-091-6

First E-book Publication: October 2013
First Print Publication: January 2014

Cover design by Dawné Dominique
Edited by Stephanie Balistreri
Proofread by Ariana Gaynor

PUBLISHER
Secret Cravings Publishing
www.secretcravingspublishing.com

Dedication

For Kimberly Hill and Mayas Sanders.
Thanks for being such great fans!

FOR THE LOVE OF A COWBOY

Cowboy Dreamin' 3

Sandy Sullivan

Chapter One

The music coming through the bar doors as they swung open, had Paige Tyler tapping her boot clad feet to the beat as she pulled her Harley to the curb. A knowing smile flirted at her lips when she heard low whistles and cat calls from a group of men nearby. No doubt they were liking how the soft leather bustier she wore pushed her breast up in an enticing display. The matching pants that went with it, hugged her ass just right and showed off how long her legs were. The whole outfit–she knew–virtually gave the impression that she could give any man she wanted the vision of a good time.

Her daddy would kill her if he saw her, but what the hell. This is why she came to Bandera to do her barhopping. No one here knew her, or her father in this small town bar that cater to the local cowboys. She glanced up at the huge neon sign of a boot with a spur hanging off its back.

Over the past few months, she'd become a regular here at The Dusty Boot. The faded wood exterior reminded her of an old western saloon with a hitching post and everything. They even had sawdust on the floor.

Her father didn't know where she went on her little excursions. He thought she spent her evenings reading to the poor little old ladies at the local nursing home, but she always took her car to the storage building where she kept her bike and clothes. After she switched out, she'd put on her helmet and hit the highway.

Another round of wolf whistles had her turning her head in the direction of a pickup truck as she removed her helmet. Damn, if she had one weakness it was a man in tight Wrangler's and dusty boots. She blew him a kiss.

"Oh, honey, come on. I'm sure you got more than that."

She cocked an eyebrow. "We'll see, cowboy." With a toss of her brown curls, she waltzed through the double doors and straight up to the bar. "Hold this back there for me, please."

"You be careful, Paige," Dan said, taking the helmet. "We got a rowdy crowd tonight."

"I'm always prepared."

"I know, honey, but I don't want to see you get hurt." He shook his finger at her, making her laugh. She loved the big, burly guy even though she hadn't known him long. He reminded her of an ex-marine with his shaved head and multiple tattoos. "Stay outta trouble, you hear me?" He'd taken it upon himself to treat her like a daughter he'd never had.

She blew him a kiss and a wink that probably drove the man crazy, but he just smiled and shook his head with a mumble of words she couldn't hear.

Thanks to all her years of Tae-Kwon-Do, she'd earned her black belt and knew how to take care of herself in any situation. She didn't use it for anything except defense, but sometimes it took a little persuasion on her part when a man got randy on her.

A crowd of dancers twirled and whirled around the dance floor in a flash of sequins and denim. She took a chair at the opposite end of the bar from the door. It helped to keep everyone in sight in case things got out of hand.

"What are ya drinkin', Paige," Peyton asked her when she approached her end of the bar.

"Hey, Peyton. Coke, please."

Peyton shook her head and laughed. "You're the only woman I know who comes to a bar dressed like that and drinks Coke."

She smiled. She sure was an enigma to most, pre-school teacher, preacher's daughter who wore leather, rode a Harley, and hung out in bars on the weekends. "I have to keep my wits about me. I just want to be around the crowd and music. I don't need the alcohol if I'm ridin'."

The woman set the glass down in front of her. Paige lifted it to her lips and took a slow sip from the straw as she turned around to take in the scenery. Several people had already paired off for the night, but there were still a few cowboys hanging around who didn't seem to be with anyone special. It didn't bother her. She wasn't here necessarily to pick anyone up. If it happened, then she'd go with the flow.

A few cowboys played pool at one of the tables set toward the back of the room while others moved in and out from the dance floor with each switch of the music. Rows and rows of tables with wooden chairs sat all over the place in various configurations depending on who moved the tables around to accommodate their group. Neon signs covered most of the walls. Everything from Bud Light to Captain Morgan lined the panels from the back of the bar to the door.

A sea of cowboy hats and rhinestones encompassed the crowd, everything from tight Wranglers to sundresses and cowboy boots. The wide variety of dress seemed funny to Paige, but she couldn't say much as she sat there in her leather.

Lots of groups laughed as they pushed each other in a joke or two. The ages ranged from early twenties to fifties. There were a few couples who seemed like then been together a long time and others who were hooking up for the night.

The normal loneliness she felt when she realized she didn't have a lot of friends, overwhelmed her for a minute. *To hell with friends. I don't need them.* The few people she still hung out with a time or two thought of her as Paige Tyler, the preacher's daughter wearing the paisley dress on Sunday with her Bible in hand, listening to the sermon like the good little girl she was supposed to be. If they saw her dressed in the leather wear she had on tonight, they'd have a frickin' heart attack.

A couple of cowboys pushed one guy back. "You're fuckin' drunk again, Jacob. Why don't you go home and sleep it off until next time."

"Leave me the fuck alone."

"You ain't worth shit anymore, man."

"Just play. I've got twenty bucks says I can beat your ass."

"I ain't takin' your money. You couldn't shoot pool right now if you tried."

"Yes, I can."

The man called Jacob got right up in the other guy's face and spit. *Oh shit.*

"You did not just fuckin' spit in my face, man."

"Yeah, I did. What are you gonna do about it?"

The bigger man pulled back his fist and hit Jacob in the stomach, doubling him over with a groan. The smaller man flew across the bar floor, sliding on his butt until he hit the wall. Paige got to her feet, moving with the crowd toward the fight. If she had to get involved, she would. Even though the one called Jacob deserved to get his ass kicked, she wouldn't allow the bigger man to beat the shit out of him especially if it got to be two against one. As he shook his head to clear it, two guys picked him up and the third punched him in the stomach.

Oh hell no.

"Paige?" the bartender pulled her back by the arm as she surged forward. "Leave them alone."

"It's three against one, Dan. I can't have that." She pushed through the crowd. "Hey, asswipe!"

The bigger guy turned around, squinting as he looked through the crowd. He was huge. His biceps bulged as he clamped his hand into a fist. Blond hair peeked out from beneath a straw cowboy hat. His blue eyes narrowed into slits. "Who said that?"

"Me, fucktard."

The man looked straight at her and laughed a gut rolling belly laugh. "You? Baby, step aside and let the men handle this."

That kind of reaction usually pissed her off, but not tonight. Dumbass didn't know what he had on his plate now that she'd decided to step in between him and drunk he wanted to beat the shit out of. "Not three on one, you aren't."

"And what the hell are you gonna do about it, baby doll?" His gaze slid over her attire as he grinned wide enough she caught a glimpse of the gold teeth in his mouth. "Your leather outfit is hot, I'll give ya that, but leave this to us men." He spun around to face his two friends.

"Bring it on, big man." She needed the man to make the first swing. It went against her grain to hit someone first. She motioned with her hands to bait him.

He laughed as he stepped closer. "I don't hit women."

"Come on, goliath. You too much of a pussy?"

"What did you call me?"

"Pussy."

The laughter from the crowd had the man's face turning purple. Their amusement died when he took a swing at her. Her first pass of her boot caught the man in the chin, splitting his lip open in a gush of blood. The next kick swiped his feet out from under him, laying him out cold on the floor.

The other two men dropped the drunk guy on the floor before backing away. "We don't want no trouble."

"You got trouble when you ganged up on one man," she said stepping in front of the man they'd called Jacob. "You okay?" she asked him without taking her eyes off the other three.

"I think I'm gonna be sick." He rolled over and pushed to his feet. The crowd parted like the Red Sea as he rushed for the bathroom, almost losing his footing a couple of time.

She cringed when she heard him puke in the hallway.

"I suggest you three take it somewhere else."

Dan pushed through the throng and appeared at her side "Yeah. Out you two. I don't want any more trouble." He motioned to the man on the floor. "Take your buddy and go."

"You ain't kickin' her and Jacob out?"

"She didn't do nothin' but stand up to you three bullies. You knew Jacob was messed up as usual, but you took advantage of him anyway."

She rolled her eyes as she heard the man heave again. She'd seen him here before, but he'd always been the quiet drunk in the corner. Yeah, she'd noticed him, all six-feet-plus of him, dark hair, built like a man who did a lot of physical labor. He'd never bothered her or anyone else, just drank his beer until he got wasted enough someone who knew him took him home or wherever. She hoped the man didn't drive like that. There'd been a time or two she'd thought about approaching him for a one night stand, but she'd always changed her mind at the last minute, unsure of whether he might be a mean drunk or just a quiet one.

He pushed his way back to the edge of the crowd as he wiped the puke from his face. "Thanks."

She winced as she glanced at the front of his shirt. "No thanks needed."

With his hat in his hand, he nodded to her and headed for the door.

Oh hell no, he isn't drivin' like this. "Where ya goin', cowboy?" she asked walking up behind him to tap him on the shoulder.

"Home," he mumbled as he pushed his hat on his head with one hand while reaching for his keys with the other.

"You ain't drivin'." She snatched the keys from him and spun out of reach. She wasn't a small woman by any means, but the man still had her by several inches.

"Yeah, I am. I'm fine." He reached for the keys, but she stuck them in her front jeans pocket.

"Buddy, you're so drunk you can't see straight."

He laughed. "I ain't that drunk. I only see two of you, not three this time." The laughter burbling from his lips sounded strained, like he hadn't laughed in a long time.

"What kind of vehicle do you drive?" she asked, sliding underneath his arm to wrap it around her shoulder. *Why the fuck do I get myself into these messes?* They walked into the cooler air of the early spring evening.

"Black Ford truck, why?" he asked, stumbling beside her.

"'Cause I'm takin' your ass somewhere so you can sleep off this drunk before you drive and I can't put your ass on my bike." She glanced across the street to the small motel. Originally, the thought of getting him home consumed her, but after she thought about it, settling him in a room would be a better idea. "Come on, cowboy, let's get you settled for the night."

"Are you takin' me home 'cause I don't think I'm up to doin' anything tonight." He stumbled beside her again and she barely caught him. They almost tumbled into the street in a tangled heap. "I really need to brush my teeth."

"I bet you do." She put her arm around his waist as they walked across the street to try to steady him a bit more. Getting to the motel without laying both of them out flat on the pavement would just make her night.

"You're pretty," he said as he looked at her profile, his puke-ladened breath wafting across her nose.

She fought the bile in her throat. God, she hated when people got puking drunk. "Thanks."

"I like the tits. Are you a biker chick?"

"Sort of."

"Where ya takin' me?"

"To this motel so you can sleep off whatever the hell you drank."

"Oh good. I can't go home like this. My parents would kill me. They don't like me drinkin' so much, but I can't help it. My life is totally fucked up."

"Sorry, dude, but I'm not psychotherapist."

"I could probably use one."

"I'm sure you could." They walked in through the glass doors of the motel. She noticed a long counter to check-in and several cheap plastic chairs along the wall. *Huh, maybe they charge by the hour*. She rang the bell when no one came out to greet them for several moments. She glanced at the open doorway where a television blared in the back. "Hey! Can I get some help here?"

A large, portly man came through the doorway scratching his crotch. "What do you want?"

"A room would be great." She grimaced and rolled her eyes.

He chewed on the cigar in his mouth as he grabbed some paperwork for her to fill out from the slots in the wall. She put Jacob in one of the chairs next to the desk so she could write. His head dropped to his chest while he mumbled to himself about something or another. Once she had the forms completed, she handed the man her credit card.

When he handed her the keys, she helped Jacob to his feet with an arm around his waist, and they stumbled outside to find the room. One-twelve, one-thirteen, one-fourteen. There it was. One-fifteen. She pushed opened the door and managed to get out of the way just in time for Jacob to hit the bed in a tumble of arms and legs.

Soft snoring met her ear.

Oh hell! The man was sleeping already and he wasn't even on the bed right. She stood with her hands on her hips deciding what to do with him. She could leave him just like he was or she could at least take off his boots to make him a little more comfortable. His feet hung off the bed so her estimate of his height seemed true although she didn't know why it made an impression on her.

She pulled off his boots and placed them near the end of the bed so he could find them in the morning. After several minutes, she decided to try to straighten him out so he could at least sleep comfortably and hopefully not vomit in his sleep. She pushed and shoved on his big body until she got him into a semi-comfortable position. "It'll have to do."

Grabbing the key to the room, she pulled the door shut behind her as she pointed herself in the direction of the bar to retrieve her bike. When she walked inside, Dan waved her over to where he stood behind the bar pouring beers. "How's Jacob?"

"Sleepin' like a baby."

"What'd you do with him?

"I left him lying on a threadbare comforter in room one-fifteen."

"You took him to the motel?"

"Yeah. He was too drunk to tell me where he lived, so I figured it would be better if he sleeps off his drunk over there. I wasn't about to let him drive home. He would have killed someone. If he does this often, I'm surprised he hasn't already."

Dan poured a beer for the waitress. "I know. I usually cut him off before he gets too drunk, but we have a new waitress tonight and she kept serving him."

"Does he do this often?"

"Too often, yeah." Dan wiped at some imaginary spot on the bar while he talked.

"Man's got a drinkin' problem then."

"I'm sure there would be some who would agree with you." He shrugged. "What are you gonna do now? You drivin' home?"

"I guess. My night is kind of ruined. Hell, I might even have to find somewhere else to hang out now that the whole bar knows I can fight."

Dan leaned toward her with his hands on the bar. "Maybe, but I think you'll be fine. Besides, I'm sure Jacob will want to tell you thank you for savin' his ass."

"I doubt he'll even remember me."

"I bet he does."

She gave him a one shoulder shrug as she glanced around the room. "Whatever, Dan. Anyway, thanks for the Coke. I'll see you next week, maybe."

He handed her the helmet from under the bar as she pulled her Harley keys out of her pocket.

With a quick wave, she disappeared back outside. A shiver rolled down her arms from the night air. It sure got cold in early spring. She straddled her bike, hit the ignition and then slipped on her helmet. She needed to go back over to the room and maybe leave the cowboy a note or something so he knew his keys were on the table. Hopefully, he would figure out where he was in the morning so he could drive home. She shook her head. Leave it to her to get in a bar fight on a Friday night in a bar forty-five minutes from home when she wasn't supposed to be doing anything like this. Preacher's daughters didn't go to bars, didn't get into bar fights, and didn't save drunk cowboys from getting their ass kicked. Only Paige Tyler would.

* * * *

Jacob Young rolled over onto his back, groaning when his head felt like it was going to split in half. Sunlight poured through the dingy drapes on the cloudy windows as he peeled his grainy eyelids open far enough to see where he was. He recognized the motel. He'd spent enough weekend nights here to know the inside of this disgusting place from corner to corner.

What the hell happened? He didn't remember much. He drank way too many beers the night before and then started to play pool with some guys he knew he shouldn't have. He didn't remember much after that. How did he get to the motel, pay for a room, and get himself to bed?

He sat up and grabbed his head as it pounded out the rhythm of a set of drums. Bongo drums if he thought about it, but that hurt too. *God, I feel like shit.*

As he squinted trying to bring the room into focus, a piece of paper on the grimy table caught his attention. He blinked several times as he leaned over to grab it.

> *Jacob –*
> *No thanks needed for savin' your ass, but please make sure you don't drive until you're sober. You really need to quit drinkin'.*
> *The keys to your truck are on the nightstand.*
> *Angel*

Who the hell is Angel?

He didn't remember last night at all. Maybe the bartender could tell him. He glanced at the clock. *Fuck.* The red digits read nine. Jeff would kick his ass when he got home. It was bad enough his brother thought he drank too much, but now he had proof if he wanted it. Somebody saved his ass last night, paid for a motel and kept him from driving drunk.

Jacob looked down at himself. *What the fuck*? He picked at the dried substance and slapped his hand over his mouth before he lost what little was left in his stomach. Apparently, at some point, he'd thrown up because the stuff covered the front of his shirt.

He unbuttoned the shirt and took it off. Luckily, he was wearing a T-shirt under it. Spring usually meant colder weather, even in Bandera, Texas.

Once he found his keys and his boots, he got to his feet and headed for the bathroom. He needed to wash out his mouth. Unfortunately, this Podunk motel didn't have toothbrushes or toothpaste for their patrons. Hell, they barely had a bed.

After he took a piss and rinsed out his mouth, he pulled on his boots and stumbled into the sunny morning.

Getting home had to be the priority right now. He was actually surprised no one had called his cell phone looking for him. *Maybe they don't care anymore. This behavior has been goin' on for some time. They must realize I'll make it home eventually, right?*

He pulled the phone from his pocket and glanced at the screen. His battery was dead. No wonder no one had called him.

His truck sat in the parking lot across the street all by itself, the rest of the patrons long gone home the night before. He squinted against the sunlight as he slowly made his way to his vehicle.

The door opened with a tug of his fingers. He crawled inside and shut it behind him. The engine turned over with a twist of the key as he took a deep breath and put the truck into drive. Hangovers sucked, but he'd have to deal with it today. Hopefully, Jeff or his parents wouldn't be around to harp on him coming in late.

Saturdays should be their day off anyway. Even if Jeff worked himself until he dropped from exhaustion, it didn't mean the rest of them had to.

"Maybe since he hooked up with Terri, even big brother wouldn't come in early."

Several minutes later, he pulled up the gate of Thunder Ridge Ranch, his family's home and business. They raised cattle on the multi-thousand acre ranch they owned, but they also had opened it to guests.

He punched in the code and watched the gate slide open all the way to allow him entrance. Yeah, sitting there was a stall. But he knew he'd be in trouble, even if he had turned thirty-one not long ago. His parents still treated him like a kid, damn it!

Not stopping at the main lodge house, he drove around between the guest houses and the stable until he reached his trailer at the back of the garden. It wasn't much, but then again, he didn't want much. He didn't have a woman to come home to, so it didn't matter. A small bachelor pad was enough for him. When or if he ever found someone to settle down with, he'd ask his parents to help him build a home like Joel or Jeff had. He didn't care enough to maintain anything yet.

He pulled up in front of his place, threw the truck into park and then stepped out.

"Where the hell have you been? We've been worried sick. You didn't answer your phone or anything," his mother snapped as she rounded the back of his truck.

"Sorry, Ma."

"Where were you, Jacob?"

"I spent the night in town."

"Again? Son, what's gotten into you?"

"Nothin'."

"Honey, please talk to me. I'm worried sick about you."

She rubbed his arm. The obvious worry on her face bothered him. The last thing he wanted in this world was to hurt his parents, but things for him weren't in a good place at the moment. "It's nothin', Ma. Can't a man have a few beers without his family goin' all ape shit?"

"Jacob, please."

"I said it's nothin'."

"Fine. I'll send your father to talk to you then."

"No. I don't want to talk to him either."

She sighed as she hugged him. "I love you, Jacob."

"I know. I love you too, Ma, but really, it's nothin' you can help me with." He pushed her back by the shoulders so he could look into her eyes.

"If you would just talk about it…"

"I can't. This is something I need to deal with on my own. It's not somethin' you, Dad, Jeff or anyone else would be able to fix. I have to do it on my own."

"You're drinkin' way too much."

"I know. I'll slow down. I promise."

He could feel her gaze on his back as he headed for his single wide mobile home, opened the door and walked in. Right now his priorities were food, shower, and to brush his teeth. The grit clinging to the enamel made him want to barf again even though he had nothing in his stomach. He toed off his boots and left them in the living room while he headed to the bathroom, dropping his hat and other clothes in the hall on his way.

His stomach rolled from too much alcohol. *I need to get a grip. This shit is for the birds. I hate being sick to my stomach.*

The mirror reflected the hell he put his body through in the last several months. His dark hair lay stuck to his skull in a matted disarray of curls. Blood shot eyes reflected the hard life he'd taken up lately. His arms and chest showed the physical labor he usually performed in his everyday life, but the sallow skin told a different story. Too much alcohol had taken its toll. He hadn't been holding up his part of the ranch. He knew it deep in his soul, but the question was how to get out of the hell he was living now. He wasn't sure if he possessed the strength to face life anymore or the miserable existence his had become.

His parents were worried. He knew the whole family was concerned about him, but he couldn't seem to dig his way out.

With a turn of the handle, the shower sprayed hot water into the corner stall of his small bathroom. Once he stepped inside, he sighed with a deep, bone weary groan. Water cascaded over his head and down his chest as he leaned against the plastic wall absorbing the heat from the water.

When had everything spiraled out of control? He wasn't sure anymore. It had started out so simple.

He shook his head to erase the disturbing memories. Thinking about them right now would make him want to drink again and he couldn't—he wouldn't—not today. Maybe this would be the first day without alcohol in a long time. Today would be the turning point in his life. Today, he would be able to move on and forget the hard decision forced on him, but he would never forget. Never in a million years.

Flashes of memory pounded his skull, bombarding him with pain like he'd never felt before. It almost brought him to his knees. A brown-headed woman in a leather bustier and skin tight leather pants flew before his closed eyelids. *What the hell?* Green eyes the color of emeralds glinted dangerously as she glanced over her shoulder at him.

He massaged his head trying to bring the memory into clarity.

Booze. Lots of booze.

Pool tables.

The Dusty Boot.

It all came back with a sharp stab to his head.

The woman jumped into the fight of three on one to save his ass. The big guy had punched him in the stomach, pushing him halfway across the bar on his butt. She'd taunted the guy while Jacob sat there on the floor like a pussy. He *was* the pussy like she'd called him, not the big guy. He'd let a woman defend him. How could he do that?

His life had come full circle. Jacob Young used to be someone to fear in a bar fight. Now, a woman took care of him.

Oh God! He remembered where the puke on his shirt came from. After the punch to the stomach, he'd rush for the bathroom only to make it to the door before he threw up all the alcohol in his system as well as the nachos he'd eaten for dinner.

How humiliating.

Jacob turned off the water and wiped his face off. *What the hell have I done? I've resorted to a woman havin' to defend me in a fight when I should have been defendin' her.* "I need to find out who she is and at least apologize."

He'd never seen her before though. Who was she? Did the bartender know her? Maybe he could help him or maybe he would run into her again, but that meant going into the bar. The one place he needed to avoid.

Chapter Two

Another Friday night found Paige putting on her satin and leather to see what the bar held. Did she dare go back to The Dusty Boot to try her luck? What if she ran into the drunk? Jacob. His name was Jacob. Not that she'd forgotten really. Who was she kidding? She hadn't forgotten him all damned week. His brown eyes had haunted her from the time she'd pulled into the storage shed to deposit her bike before she went home until now.

She wanted to know how he'd faired.

The look he'd given her as she helped him across the street haunted her. He looked so lost, she wanted to take care of him.

"Bullshit on that noise." The cracked mirror inside the shed reflected her bright green eyes, red lips and high cheekbones. No one she knew would recognize her in this getup, at least no one from church or Heaven forbid, her father.

Once she walked the bike out of the shed, she slid on her helmet, hit the ignition on her Harley and slowly pulled out onto the street. Should she go to The Dusty Boot or try a different bar?

Forty minutes later, she found herself parking at the curb outside the same establishment, as music ebbed with the opening and closing of the doors. What did she hope to accomplish other than no one recognizing her from the week before? She exhaled sharply as she set the kickstand down.

"Hey baby. Weren't you here last week on this nice lookin' machine?"

"Maybe."

"I saw you pull up. Can I buy you a beer?"

"No thanks."

"Aw, come on, darlin'." The man grabbed her hand as she stepped away from the bike. "Just one. You and me can get better acquainted and maybe have us a little fun."

"I said no thanks, buddy. Let go before you lose the limb."

"Tough girl, eh?"

"More than you know. I won't tell you again to let go of my hand before I break your arm."

"Fine, fine. It ain't worth the hassle." The guy backed away with his hands in the air.

Her boots clicked as she walked toward the door ignoring the man as his cronies laughed at his expense when he joined them. It didn't matter, but she'd keep an eye on him just in case. She didn't want trouble, but it seemed to find her.

She walked to the bar to set her helmet down as she said, "Hey, Dan."

"Paige, honey. I'm glad you came back."

"Why's that."

"Jacob has been asking about you."

"Oh?"

"Yeah. Seems he remembers you to some degree and wanted to know your name. I told him I didn't know, but he's been in here every night looking for you."

"Great, just fucking dandy."

"If you don't want nothin' to do with him, just let me know. I'll take care of him."

"No, it's fine, Dan. Maybe he just wants to say thank you and it'll be the end of it."

"I hope so."

Dan stored her helmet beneath the bar as she walked to the end and found her favorite spot open.

Peyton was tending her end of the long mahogany. "What are you drinkin', Paige, or do I have to ask."

"You don't have to ask, do you?"

Peyton laughed as she slid a tall Coke toward Paige. "No." Moving closer, she stuck two cherries in the glass. "Dan tell you Jacob has been here lookin' for you?"

"Yeah."

"He's sittin' in the corner near the back." Peyton glanced over Paige's shoulder. "I think he spotted you."

"Let's get it over with, I'd say." She spun around only to come face to chest. She glanced up at the face she couldn't forget. "Hello." Tall. Six-foot-four, at least, of pure muscle stared back. Dark hair peeked out from beneath his straw cowboy hat and the deepest brown eyes she'd ever seen on a man looked right into hers. She cocked her head to the side when she noted no alcohol coming from his breath, just a clean, refreshing minty smell. *Interesting.*

"Hi. I'm Jacob Young."

"Nice to meet you, Jacob Young."

"And you are Angel?"

She grinned thinking about the name she'd put on the note she'd left on the nightstand at the motel. "Angel is a nickname. My real name is Paige."

"Nice name. It fits you."

"Thanks. My dad thought so I guess."

Taking off his hat, he twisted the brim in his fingers. “I hoped I’d see you again. I needed to say thank you.”

“For what?”

The girl sitting on the stool next to her left, so he took the seat as she spun around to face him. “Savin’ my ass last week.”

“I didn’t do anything.” She sipped her soda.

“Yeah, you did. My memory is kind of cloudy about the particulars, but you kept those guys from killin’ me and then took me to the motel across the street to keep me from drivin’.”

“You remember quite a bit then, Jacob.”

“Where did you learn to fight?”

“Tae-Kwon-Do lessons for way too many years.”

“Ah.” He glanced at her glass as she drained it, then signaled for the bartender. “Another of whatever the lady is drinkin’ and Coke for me.”

“Two Cokes, comin’ up.”

“You aren’t drinking tonight, Jacob?”

He dropped his gaze to his hands, slipped his hat back on his head and then looked at her. “No. Funny really. After the trouble last week, I haven’t had a drop since. I have you to thank for that too, I guess.”

“Listen. I’m not sure what got you drinking so heavy in the first place and I hope what happened last week opened your eyes, but I didn’t do anything.”

“Yeah, you did. You showed me how destructive my life had become over something I really didn’t have a lot of control over.” He reached over to squeeze her fingers.

Goose bumps rose on her arm, making her frown. She'd never had a reaction like that over a man's touch before. Calluses scraped against her skin. He worked for a living apparently.

"Sorry. I didn't mean to be forward."

"It's okay." She sipped her drink. "What got the fight started last week anyway, if I might ask?"

"Somethin' stupid, really. I challenged them to some pool for money thinkin' I could win back what I'd lost at darts, but I was too drunk to even shoot the cue."

She thought about the puke on his shirt and grimaced. "Yeah, you were pretty drunk."

"Unfortunately, I've been more or less in the same condition for the last several months."

"Too bad."

"Yeah, but I think things are turnin' around. Like I said, I haven't had a drink in a week."

"Great. I'm glad."

"The best thing is, I don't want one. I've been in this bar every night since last week waitin' for you to show up and it hasn't bothered me not to drink. I've watched others actin' really stupid and I realize now how senseless the whole ritual is." He drank half his drink and then set the glass back down. "You don't drink when you come in here?"

"No. I lost my mother to a drunk driver seceral years ago so I refuse to drink and drive. If I drink, I bring a driver with me, but since I'm on a bike, it's hard to bring someone who can ride."

"What kind of bike?"

"Harley Softail."

Jacob whistled through his teeth. "Wow. Nice bike."

"You know Harleys?"

"Yeah. I don't own one, but I've had my eye on one for a long time. Money has been an issue."

"I know the feeling. They aren't cheap toys."

"No, no they aren't."

The band struck up a haunting melody in a little two-step rhythm. "Would you like to dance?"

She tipped her head to the side and smiled. He really seemed like a nice guy when he wasn't sloshed off his ass. "Sure."

He took her hand sending goose bumps racing up her arm again. Her whole body exploded in the annoying little bumps. The feeling seemed weird, but nice. Maybe it wasn't a bad thing after all. She wouldn't mind gettin' down and dirty with a nice lookin' cowboy.

Paige wasn't small by any means at five foot eleven, but this devastatingly gorgeous cowboy even towered over her.

When they reached the dance floor, he turned around to face her with a saucy little grin on his lips. He swept her into his arms as he began to two-step her around the dance floor.

"I guess I should have asked if you know how to two-step."

"Yeah, I do," she said, getting into the rhythm he created with the shuffle of his feet. The man was good. Solid muscle bunched and rolled beneath her fingers resting on his right shoulder. His hand clasped hers in his left as they scooted around the wooden floor.

"Do you come here often?"

"I have recently. I just found this place a few months ago."

"You aren't from Bandera, are you? I would remember if I'd see you around."

"No. I live in San Antonio."

"Why Bandera to come to a bar then? Surely there are a few honky-tonks in San Antonio."

The devilish grin returned. What did she say to that? She sure couldn't tell him the truth. *I'm a preacher's daughter and I can't be seen anywhere in San Antonio without my dad hearing about it. He'd have a stroke if he saw me dressed like this.* "I don't like the bars there. I found this one on one of my rides. It's quaint."

"Quaint, huh?"

She nodded as she realized he was backing her into a corner with all this talk, feeling her up for information on a personal level. "What about you? Do you frequent The Dusty Boot a lot?"

"I have in the past, but I won't be anymore."

"You're givin' it up?"

"Yes. I need to get my life together. I've taken the first step by quitting drinking."

"That's a great thing, Jacob. I'm glad you've seen the destructive power of drinking. You had me worried last week when you wanted to drive."

"I'm sorry. I should never have put you in a position to have to take care of me."

"I would have done it for anyone."

"Really?"

"Yeah. I tend to take care of people."

The music changed into a slow song, but he didn't release her. In fact, he pulled her closer and slowed their steps. "I'm glad you did it for me. Maybe I can return the favor some time."

"Maybe."

"Would you like to get a cup of coffee?"

"Are you asking me on a date, cowboy?"

He grinned. "Maybe."

"In that case, no."

"No?"

"I don't date my rescued victims."

"Okay. One friend to another then?"

"How about a Coke and a piece of pie?"

"Sounds like a date to me."

"No. No dates remember?"

"All right. Two friends havin' a piece of pie and somethin' to drink."

She stepped out of his arms, but frowned at the loss of his heat. "I'll go for that."

"What's wrong?"

"Nothin'. Why?"

"You were frownin'."

"I thought of somethin'."

"What?"

"I don't know you very well. Should I really be havin' coffee and pie with you?" she asked, coming up with something fast as an excuse rather than telling him she frowned because she didn't want to leave his arms.

"I'll be a perfect gentleman. I swear." He took her hand again. "I'd like to get to know you a little, Paige. You saved my life."

"I wouldn't go so far as to say that."

"I would. I might have killed someone if you hadn't kept me from drivin' home."

"You'd been lucky up until then."

"I know. I'd done a lot of things in the last few months I haven't been proud of." He tucked her hand in the crook of his arm to escort her to the door. "We can have pie at the diner two doors down."

"Are they open?"

"Yeah, for a little bit yet." He winked. "I know the owner." They chatted about Bandera as he told her he'd lived there most of his life. "My parents moved here when I was little."

"They live around here?"

"Yeah. We own a cattle ranch and guest place outside of town."

"Nice. Do you have siblings?"

"Yep. Eight brothers, one sister-in-law and one live-in partner for my eldest brother."

"Live-in partner? Like is he gay or somethin'?"

Jacob laughed. The sound sent chills down her back. The low, intense chuckle sounded rough like he hadn't done it in a while. "No. He just settled down with a great girl, but they aren't married or anything. They're livin' together with his son and she found out she's pregnant right around Christmas."

"Congratulations to them."

"They are pretty excited about it. My parents are too. They'll have another grandchild to love."

"Sounds like a great group."

"It's interesting livin' out there."

"Do you all live together?"

"Sort of. We all have our own places if we want or we can stay in the main house where my parents have their place. We all got deeded a piece of the home place when we turned eighteen."

"How generous of your family."

"For now, we all work together and split the profits as well as the bills."

They reached the diner and he pulled open the door.

"Hey you."

"Hey, Ann."

"What are you doin' around here this late?"

"I have a lady friend I met at The Dusty Boot and we were going to see if we could sneak a piece of your great pie and some coffee."

"Sure, honey. Have a seat anywhere. I was just cleanin' things up to close."

"Oh, don't bother on our part," Paige said. "If you're gettin' ready to close, we can go somewhere else."

Ann chuckled as she waved them into a booth. "Honey, there ain't nothin' else open this time of night in Bandera except the bar and my little diner."

"I don't want to put you out or anything."

"It's no bother. I have a fresh pot of coffee I just made and the pie only takes a minute to dish up. What kind can I get you?"

"Paige?"

"Cherry or apple with a little ice cream if you have it."

"'Course, honey. Jacob?"

"Same for me."

"Comin' right up."

They took a seat across from each other as she glanced around the diner. The décor was simple but homey with the stools sitting along the counter and the booths with their gleaming tables. "This is a cute place."

"I'll pass it along to my aunt."

"She's your aunt?"

"Yeah, my mom's sister. She never had kids of her own so she adopted all of us."

"That's right. You have a huge family."

"What about you?"

"Just me and my dad."

"I bet it was interesting growing up an only child."

"Just like I bet it was interesting growing up with eight brothers."

"Touché."

Ann brought two cups of coffee along with some cream and the pieces of pie piled high with ice cream. "Good Lord, I'll never eat all of that."

"Oh sure you will. Little thing like you—"

Paige laughed out loud. "Little? I haven't been called little since I was twelve with my height."

"You ain't that tall to me, honey. Nina and I are pretty tall too and all the boys are six foot or better."

"Six four," Jacob said, with a grin. "I like my women tall."

Her heart tripped over itself in a funny beat as she raised one eyebrow. "I ain't your woman, cowboy."

He shrugged with a grin. "Okay. I like my dance partners tall."

"Ya got me there."

They continued talking about little things. Bandera and how the town had changed in the years he'd grown up there. San Antonio's differences as well.

"Did you grow up in San Antonio?" he asked as the fork disappeared between his full lips.

Why was she thinking about what it might feel like to have those tempting, kissable lips on hers? She didn't need his kind of trouble and trouble he would be from what she'd seen of him. "No. My dad is a pre—" *Shit.*

"A what?"

She bit her lip, debating on whether to tell him the truth or not. Surely he wouldn't know her daddy, would he? "He's a preacher." A roar of laughter erupted from his mouth as he almost choked on his pie. "I didn't think it was that funny."

"Oh my God. That's priceless!"

"Jacob," she growled in warning. A warning he didn't heed.

"He's a preacher? I bet he doesn't know his little girl dresses in a leather outfit and rides a Harley either."

"No he doesn't. He would have a stroke if he knew, so just hush about it."

Jacob coughed several times to clear his throat. "Where does he think you go on the weekends?" He raised his hand to stop her words. "Wait. Let me guess. The hospital?"

She sighed in a rush. "A nursing home to read to the older ladies."

"My, my. The preacher's daughter is a little liar."

"Do you really think I could tell my father I want to ride a motorcycle, dress in leather and have sex with random men?"

"You do?"

"Sometimes, yeah, but I sure as hell can't tell him what I do on my weekends."

"How do you get away with it? He doesn't know you own the bike, *huh*."

"No. I keep it and my clothes in a storage shed." She scooted out of the booth. "Forget it. Why I'm even telling you this is beyond me. Just forget I ever told you anything. You don't know me. I don't know you." She headed for the door. "Think of it this way, Jacob. We never met." She pushed open the door and headed back down the sidewalk to retrieve her helmet. This whole night was a mistake.

She should never have helped him. She should have let him get his ass kicked and drive home drunk. *And if he would have killed someone or himself, I would have felt like shit.*

"Paige, wait!" He caught up with her as she pulled open the door to the bar. "Come on, Paige. I'm sorry. It's not funny. I'm sure you have your reasons for doing what you do. You aren't really any different than me."

"I'm a lot different than you, Jacob. I don't get drunk to drown my sorrows and forget about things or whatever the hell the reason you were drinkin' like a damned fish for. I face my problems."

"Face them? You call hiding yourself from your father facing your problems?"

"Don't judge me, mister."

He grabbed her arm. "I'm not, Paige. I'm trying to understand."

"What the fuck do you care?" She yanked her arm out of his grasp. "You've got your own issues."

"Yeah, I do and I'm learning to face them."

"By drinkin' yourself into stupor?"

"I'm sorry you had to see me like that."

"It doesn't matter." She shoved her way into the building and headed for the bar. "Can I have my helmet, please?"

"Don't go, Paige."

"We're done, Jacob."

"I'm afraid if you leave, I'll never see you again."

"What part of we're done don't you get?"

Chapter Three

Paige. Paige *what*? He didn't know and it was pissing him off. Jacob tossed a bale of hay from the door of the loft into the stack near the wall, one right after the other until sweat poured down his back.

She'd hopped on her bike and tore out of the parking lot of the bar like her ass was on fire and he wished he'd followed her or knew her last name for God's sake! Maybe he could find out from the bartender. The guy seemed to be friendly with her.

He wiped the sweat from his forehead with the back of his shirt sleeve before settling his straw cowboy hat back on his head. He was tired and he wanted a drink, but he wouldn't. Drinking was a thing of the past for him. It sure as hell didn't solve anything in his life so he figured it wouldn't do him any good now. Didn't mean he didn't want one though.

"Jacob, you up there?"

"Yeah, Dad."

"Can you come down here a minute? I need to ask you something."

"Sure. I'll be right down." He slipped off his work gloves and laid them on the next hay bale ready to be moved. The ladder to the bottom of the barn stood back to his right, outlined by the hole in the floor leading down. When he reached it, he hopped down the rungs, taking one at a time until he reached the floor beneath. "What's up?"

"I just wanted to talk to you about your drinking."

"I've given it up, Dad."

"I know you have, son, and I wanted to say how proud I am of you. You've taken steps to change your behavior. It's commendable." His dad dropped his hand onto Jacob's shoulder.

It had been a long time since he thought his father might be proud of him. Being the third eldest of nine boys, he sometimes felt like he got lost in the shuffle of not being the oldest.

"I don't know what made you start in the first place, but I'm glad you found something to help you stop."

"A woman, both times, Dad."

"I'm sorry to hear that, but I'm glad whoever helped you quit was there. Is it someone we might meet someday?"

"I doubt it. I've only met her twice myself."

"I see."

"No, you probably don't, Dad. You see a couple of weeks ago, I almost got my ass kicked in a bar fight over a game of pool. A tall, slender woman jumped into help me, taking the biggest of the guys down with a couple well placed kicks. His friends bailed the minute they saw what she could do, I guess." He shrugged and then readjusted his hat. "I made a fool of myself in front of her and several other people by throwing up everything I had in my stomach outside the bathroom door at The Dusty Boot. Instead of leaving me there to wallow in puke or drive myself home drunk off my ass, she paid for a motel room."

"Wow."

"Yeah."

"Do you know who she is?"

"Sort of. I spent last week at the bar hoping she'd show up so I could tell her thank you. Funny thing was, I saw how stupid people were acting with alcohol in their system and I realized I'd been acting the same way. I haven't had a drink since the night she helped me."

"Interesting way to quit drinking."

"Yeah. I'm not sure why it made such an impression on me, but it did."

"Did you find out who she is?"

"Yeah. I met her two nights ago again. We had coffee and pie with Ann at the diner. When we got to talkin', I found out she's a preacher's daughter."

"And she's hanging out at bars?"

"Yep."

"Interesting."

"I know."

"So what's her name?" his dad asked, propping himself against the stall door like he didn't plan to go anywhere anytime soon.

"Paige, but I don't know her last name. All I know is her father is a preacher in San Antonio, but there are thousands of churches there." He wiped the sweat from his neck, realizing his T-shirt was stuck to his back. Didn't matter. Work needed to be done. Sweat came with the job of handling cattle or running a ranch. "I'm hoping to talk to the bartender to see if he knows her last name, of course he wouldn't even tell me he knew her when I asked him the first time. I think he's protecting her a bit."

"How are you gonna find her?"

Jacob crossed his arms over his chest. "I don't know, Dad, but I have to. I need to see her again."

"It sounds like you're a bit intrigued by this girl."

"Yeah, sort of. I'm not sure what it is about her."

"Whatever it is, I'm glad for it."

"Me too. But I really don't want to get involved with another woman right now."

"Want to talk about it?"

"I can't. It's a situation forced on me a while back and it's somethin' I'm gonna have to live with for the rest of my life."

"I hope you know me and your mother are always here for you, Jacob."

Jacob wrapped his dad in a hug before he stepped back. "I know, Dad, but this is somethin' I don't think you or Mom would ever forgive me for."

"We would forgive you anything, son."

"This wouldn't be easy for either of you."

"Try us."

"I can't right now, Dad. Maybe someday I can come to grips with what I've done, but for now I'm strugglin' with it every day."

"Well, I hope you find your lady friend."

"I hope so too. I'm not goin' back to the bar until this weekend. Hopefully, she'll show up, but I'm not holdin' my breath. She was pretty mad at me."

"I think she'll be over it and be willin' to talk to you. You're a handsome fellow."

"Looks don't always make it easier."

"You'll do fine, son."

"I hope so. I really want to get to know her a little better, you know, as a friend. I think she'd be a great person to be friends with."

"Friends, *huh*?" The grin on his dad's face told Jacob he didn't buy that explanation at all.

Jacob smiled. "Well, maybe friends with benefits."

"I bet." His dad clapped him on the back. "I'll see you at dinner."

"Thanks for the talk."

"You're welcome, Jacob. Anytime."

Jacob climbed the ladder into the loft to get back to work. The hay wouldn't stack itself. He could have left it for Jeff or Joey, but he wanted the physical labor to keep him sane. Hard work never hurt anyone.

A low, masculine laugh followed by a high pitched giggle, made him pause. Joel and Mesa or Jeff and Terri?

In the tack room.

Jeff and Terri.

"Hard, baby?"

"Like a damned rock. It sucks we have to sneak into the barn to have a little alone time."

"Ben has been hard to deal with lately."

"And your pregnancy isn't makin' this any easier."

"Aw, poor baby. You'll live."

The soft feminine laugh made him smile. Jacob took a seat on the hay bale, not wanting to disturb his brother and his girl if they were going to have a little fun. Maybe someday he'd find a woman to have a serious relationship with, but he wasn't sure. The situation with Veronica soured him on relationships. Her situation and the subsequent decision they made together didn't make him want a connection on a serious level with any woman. The minute everything had taken a turn, she'd basically bailed on him and found someone else.

Funny thing? Most of the women in Bandera were trying to get their claws into any of the Young brothers, but Veronica didn't want to turn her relationship into marriage with him. He'd asked. She'd turned him down flat.

His thoughts turned to Paige. *What would she be like in the sack*? She seemed rough around the edges. Her personality was a little persnickety. He wanted to get to know her better, he knew that much, but how much better? *Huh*. He wasn't sure.

Her emerald green eyes were gorgeous. Her tall, slender body could melt chocolate on a winter's day. The way she handled herself with men left a little to be desired. She said she was into random sex though. There might be something there. He could use a good lay. It had been a long time since he'd had meaningless sex with someone. Paige might be up for something along those lines if he could ever figure out her last name or get a phone number.

Damn.

Well, nothing he could do about it right at the moment.

He'd heard the door to the tack room close and lock a few minutes ago, so he figured it would be safe enough to go back to work even though he could still hear his brother's sighs and Terri's groans. Listening to someone else have sex wasn't good for his libido. He wanted that. He wanted a warm pussy around his cock. Just the thought of licking juices from Paige, made him hard as a brick.

Maybe he'd take a trip into town tonight to see if he could find a random woman. No, the thought soured his stomach. He wanted Paige in a leather bustier, little leather G-string and those fuck me boots she wore the other night. *Oh yeah.* He could do her in a minute. Was she into rough sex? He sure hoped he could find out and soon. Tonight, it would be a cold shower and his slicked up hand. By this weekend, he'd know her name and where to find her or he'd damn sure die trying.

* * * *

Paige smoothed the paisley dress down as she took her place in the pew for her father's Saturday evening service. *Just a little longer and I can make my getaway.*

After spending time with Jacob last week, she'd been restless. She smoothed the material around her thighs again as her toes tapped out an unheard rhythm inside her short-heeled pumps. No fuck me boots this evening. She sighed. This service couldn't be over fast enough for her. She needed to feel the wind on her face.

"And God said…"

Oh, Lord help me.

Her father droned on and on. Most of his sermon seemed lost on her as her thoughts drifted to last week.

She really shouldn't have taken off like she did, but Jacob's words hit too close to home. Was she really running from her problems with her father like he suggested?

Nah.

Well, maybe.

Okay, yes, but that didn't mean he knew anything about her or her father. Their relationship was a strained one on a good day. If he knew about her bike and her weekend trips, he'd disown her. She couldn't have that now could she? He was all she had these days with her mother resting beneath the big oak tree in the church cemetery. God, she missed her some days. What would her mother think of her riding a Harley and dressing in leather? Maybe she needed to spend a little time out there tomorrow after church.

Tonight she needed something.

Jacob.

Why?

She wished she knew. What was it about the troubled cowboy that drew her to him like a moth to flame?

The Dusty Boot would be her destination. In one way, she hoped Jacob was there to greet her. In another, she hoped he wasn't. Maybe some random guy would work better. No, she wanted Jacob.

Mrs. Robertson patted her hand and smiled. "He does drone on, doesn't he?"

"Sometimes."

"I'm not sure how you do it, child."

She smiled and shook her head. "I don't know either most days."

"God love the man."

"I'm sure he does."

"Visited your momma lately?"

"No, I was just thinking about goin' out there tomorrow after services."

"Good idea. You look like you need a good mother daughter talk."

"And Jesus rose up…"

"Oh brother," Mrs. Robertson said as Paige giggled under her breath earning a stern look from her father.

"Let us pray."

"Thank goodness," Mrs. Robertson added.

Paige smothered another laugh with a cough.

The moment services let out, she headed next door to the church where she and her father lived. The quaint little white house had been home for several years now with the swing on the front porch and the flowerbeds she loved to tend. White curtains adorned the two front windows, now closed against the winter winds. Early spring in San Antonio could still be rather cold in the evenings even being in south Texas. The days were mild with temperatures in the fifties or sixties, but nights grew cold when the sun went down.

"Paige?" her father called several minutes later.

"Yes, Papa?"

"There you are." He patted her shoulder as he headed for the kitchen. He usually took a nip before bed from the whiskey bottle he kept in the cupboard above the refrigerator. She pretended not to notice. "Are you headed to Sunnyside?"

"Yes."

"I'm sure the ladies love havin' you there to read to them every weekend. You're such a good child."

If you only knew. "I'll be home late. Don't wait up." She knew he wouldn't. His nip of whiskey usually meant half the bottle and resounding snores by the time she came home.

"Be careful."

"I will." She grabbed her purse, the keys to her small sedan and a jacket to ward off the chill of the coming night until she reached the storage shed where her bike sat. Good thing the place gave the tenants the code to get into the gates. She could come and go as she pleased.

Several minutes later, she punched in the code and watched as the gate swung open. One-forty-two. There it was. Her lifeline to the outside. Her private domain for her *other* personality. Will the real Paige Tyler come on down!

She shut off the engine of her car and stepped out. The wind chilled her arms, but she didn't care. The wind would feel good on her face. There wouldn't be a leather bustier tonight, but her leather jacket would cut the chill in the air as she rode.

The lock gave way under her fingers. She lifted the roll door of the shed and then flipped on the bare light bulb in the center of the room. The Harley Softail sitting in the center of the storage unit made her smile. *All mine.* Every inch of the gleaming bike belonged to her and she loved it like a child. "Aw, baby. I'm sorry I haven't been here in a few days, but we'll be ridin' the wind shortly."

The door rolled back down with a push of her hand until it banged against the concrete floor. Goose bumps pebbled her flesh as she stepped out of her dress to reveal her lacy strapless bra and G-string underwear. She loved sexy underwear and the men she ended up with usually liked them too. She giggled. Would Jacob? She hoped he was at the bar tonight. She needed his hunky self to scratch the incredible itch she'd developed since she met him.

She pulled on the white tank top from the dresser and her skin tight leather pants. Her fuck me boots sat in the corner waiting for her to slip them on. What about fucking with just the boots on? *Wow. That would be really hot.*

She lifted the door on the storage shed again before she straddled her bike and slipped on her helmet. Once she pushed it out into the open, she tapped the ignition to start the bike.

The distinctive Harley growl made her smile. Lord, she loved that sound. She could almost come from the rumbled of the bike between her legs.

Once she was outside the door, she stored her purse and keys in the saddle bags and then locked the storage shed with a snick of the lock. Her car would be safe until she returned.

The tires hummed under the machine as she headed down Interstate 10. Cars zipped past her, but she didn't pay any attention to them. The destination she had in mind took up her entire thought process or more like the man she hoped to find there invaded her thoughts to overwhelming. Why was she so stuck on him? What made him so special? Was it the sadness in his eyes or the overwhelming need to take care of him she felt every time she got near him?

She wasn't sure. Maybe fucking him once would take care of those thoughts.

It wouldn't hurt anyway.

Before she knew it, she was pulling down the side street in Bandera where The Dusty Boot parking lot took up one whole block. The music could be heard with each swing of the doors.

The parking lot overflowed with trucks and cars of every shape and size. She couldn't tell if Jacob was there or not since there were several trucks matching the description of his.

I hope he's here.

Once she got inside the bar, she found Dan behind the mahogany expanse and waved. “Hey, Dan.”

“Hey, Paige. I didn’t think you’d be here this weekend after the way you left last Saturday.”

“I know, but I couldn’t stay away from your handsome face.”

“Yeah, right. Mimi would believe that like she would believe one of these hot young cowboys was comin’ onto her.”

Paige laughed. Mimi was Dan’s wife, stood about four foot nothing and weighed in at about two hundred pounds. Don’t piss the woman off though or she’d take out your knees before you could blink. She took no shit off anyone, especially her husband, the big tough biker dude.

Dan put her helmet beneath the bar before he wiped down an imaginary wet spot with the towel in his hand. “He’s here you know.”

“He?” she asked, pretending to be nonchalant about what she wanted.

“Jacob.” Dan cocked his head to the side, indicating the back corner of the bar to his right.

“Why would you think I’m lookin’ for him?” Paige picked at the imaginary lint on her top, leaving the zipper open on the front of her jacket.

“I saw you two last week. You can’t put anything over on this old fella, Paige. You two are hot for each other. I saw the way you was dancin’.”

“It’s nothin’, Dan. Just gratitude on his part.”

“I don’t believe a word you is sayin’, darlin’.”

Paige took the Coke Dan set out and moved down to the other end of the bar to her normal spot. Amazing, it always seemed to be open when she got there. With her back to where Jacob sat, she concentrated on the music, letting it surround her with the beat.

The band they had in here every Saturday night actually sounded pretty good. Maybe someday they'd make it big in Nashville. She hoped so. The members were nice people.

She waited knowing sooner or later Jacob would approach her.

Her skin tingled from the heat of his gaze.

She wondered if he'd started drinking again. She knew how hard it was to give up a habit.

Several minutes later, the warmth of his breath on the back of her neck told her he stood near. "Paige."

Goose bumps flittered across her arms at the sound of his voice. She closed her eyes to absorb his heat before she turned to face him. Her whole body exploded in sensation the moment she met his gaze. "Jacob."

He leaned in to talk in her ear. "I'm glad you're here."

"Are you?" she asked, fighting the urge to rub herself all over him.

"Yeah. I prayed I'd see you again."

"Why?"

"I wanted to apologize for my behavior last week."

So it's all about his behavior and not really his need to see her again. Disappointment surrounded her heart. She'd really hoped he wanted to see her for other reasons. "Apology accepted." She spun back around to face the bar.

"I'm not done."

"I am." She shot over her shoulder. *Why am I doin' this? If he's sincere in his apology, which I think he is, why am I givin' him such a hard time?*

He took her arm and spun her back around on the bar stool. The next thing she knew his mouth slammed down on hers in a desperate kiss that pushed her back against the bar. Even though the kiss was harsh and demanding, she dove into it with all the pent up desire in her body for this man. Her hands found the front of his shirt as she grasped the material in her fists to pull him closer. She spread her thighs to take him between them as he deepened the kiss to volatile.

She didn't taste alcohol on his tongue, just man and desire.

He pushed his hands into her hair, fisting the strands at the back of her head. God, she loved a man to take control.

When he finally pulled back, she could see the need in his eyes as he stared down at her.

"Wow."

"Pretty good for a cowboy."

"You ain't seen nothin' yet, darlin'." He glanced around them for a minute. "Care to get out of here?"

"What are you askin'?"

"I'd like to take our kiss a bit further if you're game."

"Oh, I'm game all right."

"We can go back to my place. It's not far. About ten minutes."

Did she really want to get personal with this man on the level of seeing his bachelor pad or would it be better to get a motel in town. She cringed at the thought of the seedy place across the street. She wanted a little more pampering from this man for the hell he'd put her through the last couple of weeks. He'd better live up to the desire she saw in his eyes. "Sure."

"You can either follow me back to the ranch or you can ride with me."

"I'll follow you." She hopped off the stool and followed him toward the door. Dan already had her helmet out sitting on the edge of the bar as she rounded the end. He smiled and winked. "I don't want to hear anything out of you."

"I didn't say a word."

"Good." She tucked her helmet under her arm. Letting Jacob chase after her, she pushed open the door and headed for her bike.

Minutes later she found herself tooling along a dirt road behind a black truck. The gate to the ranch came into view to the right. Jacob pulled up and punched in a code allowing the gate to swing open.

She followed him down the long driveway. Several double cabins stood off to the right and a huge main house stood silhouetted in the moonlight to their left. She couldn't see a lot of the place because of the darkness, but it reminded her of a typical cattle ranch. The sound of cattle mooing in the distance brought a smile to her lips. Definitely a cowboy, her Jacob. *My Jacob? What the hell?*

They continued to follow the dirt road between the cabins, past the big barn to a single wide mobile home near the back of the main lodge. It wasn't much, but what did she know. Really, she barely knew the guy. *What am I thinking?*

He stopped his truck near the small steps leading inside as she pulled up next to him. She really hoped the loud bike hadn't awakened anyone on the ranch. It wasn't every day someone on a Harley drove onto a cattle ranch.

She shut the bike off and pushed down the kickstand, letting it lean to the left.

"Someday you'll have to take me on your bike," he said, stopping next to her as she pulled off her helmet.

"Maybe."

"You can leave your stuff out here. No one will mess with it."

"Okay." She draped the helmet over the backseat rest. "Do you have a lot of guests?"

"Not this time of year. Most people come in the summer when it's nice and warm." He took her hand in the warmth of his own as he walked toward his home. "It isn't much."

"You're a bachelor. I wouldn't expect much."

"It's better than a dingy motel room though."

He opened the door and she got her first look at Jacob's personal space when he flipped on the light switch. A couch sat to the left, a big screen television sat to the right and a recliner took up the space next to the couch. A kitchen sat behind the living room with an open space between them. The kitchen was small, but had all the amenities from what she could tell. Not much decorated the walls, but then again she wouldn't think a single guy would have a lot of flowery pictures or anything. She did see a few photographs in frames sitting on the end tables.

"Your family?"

"Yeah. The one on the wall is all of us."

"Big family."

"Yep."

She looked closer. "Triplets?"

"Yeah. Joel, Jason and Joshua are identical triplets. Joel got married recently."

"I bet that was fun growing up."

"They were a handful as kids."

"You're the third oldest you said."

He nodded. "Jeff is the oldest."

"Wow. Nine boys. I bet your mom is completely gray."

"Actually, no. She's got beautiful long black hair."

"Do you have Native American blood?"

He pointed to the large picture on the wall. "Some, yes. You can see it more in my mother than any of us boys, although most of us have the dark hair. The triplets have blue eyes. Jeff's are grey and mine are brown like my mother's. The rest of the boys are a grouping of those three."

"What a combination."

"You could say that, yeah. It's an interesting family dynamic."

"You all seem to be close though?"

"Not always. Typical boys, you know."

She bit her lip and dropped her gaze to her feet. "Jacob, why were you drinkin' so heavily?"

He moved away from her to drop his keys and hat on the coffee table. "I don't want to talk about it."

"It would help if you did."

"No it won't. I'm past it. I'm not drinkin' anymore."

"I can see the sadness in your eyes."

"It's over. There's nothin' I can do to change what happened so I'm moving on." He stopped in front of her. "Wanna get nekkid?"

"That's what we came here for, isn't it?"

"Yeah, but all this serious talk, I thought you might have changed your mind."

"No. I want to help you for some ungodly reason."

"Nothin' to help, darlin'. It's done." He shoved his hands into her hair to tip her head back with a sharp tug on her scalp. "I'm gonna lick you all over."

"Promises, promises," she whispered as his lips did a slow crawl along her jaw to her ear.

"Not a promise, honey. It's a fact."

She found his firm chest beneath the shirt encasing it. One thing she'd noticed about him from the get-go was how toned his body was. He must do a lot of physical labor on the ranch to keep his muscles in such good shape.

"Touch me."

"Oh, I plan to, honey."

His hand encircled her breast, palming her flesh until his fingers found her nipple under her tank top. She moaned as he pinched it between his thumb and first finger. Pain along with pleasure. She couldn't get enough. Would he go for a little forceful fucking? She hoped so.

He stepped back to slowly push her jacket from her shoulders, letting it fall in a heap to the floor. "Nice. You have beautiful breasts."

"Thanks."

"Just the right size for my hands."

She placed her palm flat against his. "I like your hands. Long lean fingers. Strong. Callused."

"They might be a little rough on your skin."

"I like rough," she said, watching his eyes.

"Good. So do I."

"Make me yours for the night, Jacob."

"You got it, babe." He scooped her up in his arms before she could utter a squeak and then strolled down the hallway toward the back of the trailer.

His room wasn't much, a huge bed, a long dresser, a couple of nightstands, and nothing more. He dropped her on the mattress and covered her mouth in a desperate kiss.

"God, I want you."

"Me too."

He stood. "Undress me. Slowly."

She crawled up on her knees so she could reach the snaps on the front of his western shirt. Her fingertips tingled touching the hair roughed skin after she parted the material to reveal his chest. *Wow.* Dark, dusky nipples tempted her with their pebbled hard tips. "I want to taste you."

"Go ahead."

She skimmed her lips from the center of his chest to the right nipple, encircling it with her tongue until he moaned low in his throat. Unable to resist, she nipped it with her teeth.

"Naughty girl."

"*Mmmm.*"

As she nipped and sucked on the tip, she worked the belt buckle at his waist loose before she parted the denim material to reveal his incredible length to her touch. The man had an impressive cock although she really didn't have a lot to judge by. She talked the talk, but she hadn't really walked the walk as much as she made it sound. Her experience in the bedroom department lacked something like numbers. Oh, she wasn't a virgin by any stretch of the imagination, but she'd only been with two other men in her lifetime. Luckily, they'd both taught her something about pleasing men.

She licked her way down his washboard abs as she pushed his boxers and his jeans to the floor. "Step out."

He quickly toed off his boots and stepped out of his clothes, leaving them in a heap near the window.

"Wow. A little horny are we?"

"A lot horny, darlin'."

"God, I love when you call me that."

"What else do you like?"

"Lots of things," she said, as he stalked closer in an unhurried gate meant to tantalize her into wanting him. He didn't need to do anything of the sort. Her pussy already wept with need for this cowboy. "I wanna suck you."

"No."

"No?"

"Later, maybe." He held out his hand and she slipped her palm into his as she stood. "I'm going to undress you now."

"Okay."

He slipped the tank top over her head, leaving her standing bare from the waist up. "I love these. They're perfect."

"One is a little bigger than the other."

"Such pretty, rosy nipples."

He encircled one with his tongue like she'd done to him. Shivers skittered along her arms at the feeling of his mouth. He flicked the tip with his tongue, bringing her up on her toes. Her nipples were one of the most sensitive parts of her body. She could almost come from nipple stimulation.

"I want to put clamps on these."

"Clamps?"

"Yeah, nipple clamps with a cute little weight hanging between them. Have you ever had those on your breasts?"

"No."

"Wait here." He moved to his dresser and opened one of the drawers. A moment later, he returned with something in his hands. "I haven't used these on anyone before, just so you know."

He held up a small chain with a pinchers on each end and a small sliding ball in the middle of the chain. "You keep nipple clamps in your drawer?"

"I bought them a while back. I hadn't had anyone special I wanted to use them on, but your nipples are just right for clamps." He sucked one of her nipples hard between his lips until it stood up pointed and stiff. "Perfect." The clamp slid on with a slight twinge of pain. He tightened the end down until the pain brought tears to her eyes. "A little too much?"

"Yeah."

He loosened it slightly and then did the same to the other nipple. When he stepped back to admire his handy work, the weight hanging on the chain between her breasts pulled the clamps on her nipples until they stung.

"Okay?"

She took a deep breath and nodded.

"Good." His eyes glittered with lust. "They look fabulous on you."

"Thank you."

"Now, for the pants." He worked her belt loose before pushing her leather pants to the floor and indicating she should toe off her boots. "Are you wet?"

"God, yes."

He skimmed his hand down her abdomen, pushing his fingers between her thighs. "Soaked. You like a bit of pain with your sex, *eh*?"

"I guess. I think so. I like the way it feels when you pull my hair and take what you want."

He looked surprised. "You've been with men before, right?"

"I'm not a virgin, Jacob, although I'm not terribly experienced either."

"How many guys have you been with?"

"Two besides you."

He shoved his fingers through his hair, leaving it sticking up in several directions. "Shit."

"What?"

"I thought you had been with several guys." He moved to take the clamps off her nipples.

"No, leave them."

"They shouldn't stay on more than a few minutes especially since you've never had your nipples in clamps before. Brace yourself. This is gonna hurt."

He removed one and as the blood rushed back into the tortured tip, she hissed with the pain. He soothed it with his tongue until it no longer hurt.

"That wasn't so bad."

"I hate to be the bearer of bad news, darlin', but last time I checked, you have two of those."

"Aw, fuck!"

When he removed the second one, she cried, "Owie, owie." Again, he soothed it with his tongue, but this time her clit throbbed with the beat of her heart in the tip of her breast.

"I'm sorry."

"Don't be. I liked the way they felt while they were on."

"You do like a little pain then."

"Yeah, I guess I do." He pulled back his hand and smacked her bare ass. "What the hell was that for?"

"To see how much pain you like."

"I've never been spanked before in my life. That hurt."

"Your mom and dad never spanked you?"

"No." She rubbed the sore spot with the palm of her hand. "I was the perfect preacher's daughter, remember?"

"Ah yes. Daddy's little angel in leather."

"Don't make fun of me."

He held up his hands in a defensive posture as he backed up a little. "I'm not, honey. I think it's great how you are the little angel with a crooked halo being held up by devil's horns." He put his hands down and crooked his finger. "Come 'ere."

She tipped her chin down as one eyebrow shot up. "Why?"

"Because I wanna fuck you until the sun comes up."

She sauntered closer. "Good because I want it too."

He grabbed her around the waist and hoisted her up so she could wrap her legs around him. His cock stood hard between them.

"Condom?"

"Crap. Let me grab one out of the drawer." He set her down and walked to the nightstand drawer. After rummaging around, he cussed a blue streak.

"What's wrong?"

"I'm out apparently."

"You can't be serious."

"Dead serious."

"All wet and nowhere to go."

He held up a finger. "Let me throw some clothes on. I'll be back in a minute."

"You aren't drivin' to town to get some, are you?"

"Honey, I have eight brothers. Don't you think one of them will have a condom they can spare?"

"You are really goin' to go around to your brothers asking for a condom?"

"Do we have a choice?"

"Well yeah, I guess we do." She bit her lip. "I'm on birth control. Have you been tested lately?"

"Yeah, after my last girlfriend."

"Me too. I mean after the last guy I slept with even though he used a condom every time we were together."

"What are you sayin', darlin'?"

"I'm sayin' do you think we can skip the condom this time?"

* * * *

Should he trust her? Did he have a reason not to? She is a preacher's daughter, right?

"What's wrong?"

"I'm not sure if I should trust you."

"Seriously, Jacob?" She jammed her fists on her hips. "I can show you my birth control pills if you want. They are in my purse in my saddle bags on the bike."

"All right. I guess I don't have a reason not to trust you."

"Do you want to get laid tonight or not, big boy?"

Shivers raced down his back. "Oh, hell yeah."

"Then I guess you'll have to trust me. I mean, really. Do I have a reason to distrust you? No."

He grabbed her around the waist and tossed her on the bed. "Prepared to be fucked."

"Come and get it, handsome."

God. He loved her mouth, her tits, her ass and he was about to really love her pussy.

She scooted up on the bed until her head lay on his pillow. Her brown hair lay in a halo around her head, giving her an ethereal look. He brushed the hair off her forehead. "You're so beautiful," he whispered, in awe that such a gorgeous woman would want to go to bed with him.

"You're pretty gorgeous yourself, cowboy. I could eat you up."

"I'm gonna eat you until you scream my name."

"What was your name again?"

"You're gonna pay for that." He ran his tongue from her lips to her ear, down her neck and across her collarbone. He left a little love bite on her shoulder.

"You bit me!"

"Just a little one."

"I hope it can't be seen. My father will have a cow."

"Not unless you're naked in front of him."

"Never."

"Then you're fine. I like marking my women."

"I'm not your woman, Jacob. We've had this talk."

He kissed her quickly. “You are for tonight, honey.” He continued his journey down her chest, stopping to lick and nibble on her breasts for several minutes as she moaned under him. The little sounds she made with her arousal were music to his ears. Speaking of arousal, he could smell her sweet scent, letting it wrap around his senses.

Her abdomen quivered under his licking assault.

The thatch of hair at her pussy tickled his chin as he made his way to the treasure he sought. Eating out a woman was the best. There wasn’t anything better than sweet cum on his tongue as she came undone beneath him.

She spread her thighs, begging on whimpers for the touch of his tongue on her clit.

“Please, Jacob.”

“Please what, darlin’?”

“I want your tongue.”

“Where?” he asked, pressing his nose to the curls guarding her sweetness from his mouth.

“On my clit. God, please. I need you.”

The first swipe of his tongue had her hips coming off the bed. Moans escaped her lips as she tossed her head on his pillow. With both hands on her hips to keep her in place, he continued his assault on her clit, bringing her to a screeching orgasm within seconds. Her screams probably told the entire ranch he had a woman in here, but he didn’t care. Her satisfaction meant everything.

He continued to softly lick her clit while she came down from her high, giving her a minute to recover before he took her to the heights of ecstasy again.

“Again?”

"Oh yeah."

Her clit hardened under his tongue, waiting for the touch, friction or whatever you wanted to call it. Her pussy glistened with her cum, so he licked until every drop had disappeared. The moan that spilled from her lips made him smile. He loved taking a woman to the highs of good sex.

It took a bit longer this time and a bit more stimulation to get her there, but he managed to bring her to another orgasm with his tongue and fingers. Her pussy was so tight. He could almost believe she was a virgin. He frowned. Maybe she lied about it. Maybe she really hadn't been with anyone before. Of course, she knew a little by her actions earlier, but her hesitation with it all seemed almost virgin like.

Quit second-guessing her.

He moved so his cock was nestled in the v of her spread thighs. The sight of her pussy lured him in. He needed to feel her warmth more than he needed his next breath. Going bare with her scared him a little, but he trusted her. He didn't know why, but he did.

He sank into her warmth with a sigh. "God, you feel amazing."

"Fuck me, Jacob. I need it hard."

"Give me a minute, darlin' or this will be over before we get started."

"We can do it again. Just fuck me."

"Such dirty language from such a good girl."

She wrapped her legs around him and dug her heels into his butt, urging him on as he sank farther into her slick pussy. Her muscles quivered around him. He hit her G-spot with each slow thrust, driving her crazy with need. Her eyes were wild with desire. Her fingernails dug into his biceps as he increased the pace of his thrusts. He couldn't stop. Within what seemed like seconds, his balls drew up, signaling his imminent release. Paige screamed his name as she came apart in his arms.

"Oh God," he murmured, losing his own tempestuous hold on his desire.

Cum squirted out the end of his dick, coating both of them with his seed. It had been a long time since he'd went without a condom. He'd forgotten how awesome it felt.

"You okay?" she asked in a whisper as she reached up and kissed his chest.

"Yeah."

"That was pretty awesome, cowboy."

"You can say that again."

"That was pretty awesome, cowboy."

They laughed together, but it turned into a mutual moan as he slowly pulled out of her warm body.

"Give me a minute to recover and we can do it again."

"You're serious?"

"Of course, I am. I told you I wanted to fuck you until the sun came up. I wasn't jokin'."

"Well, you know I'd love to stay, but I really should be gettin' home. I can't stay all night, Jacob."

"I know, Paige. Your daddy would have a fit if you stayed out past midnight."

"That is the understatement of the century."

She rolled off the bed and headed for the small bathroom off to the right of his bedroom. A minute later, he heard the toilet flush and the water run in the sink while he laid there on the bed with a stupid grin on his face. Paige was the first woman he'd slept with since Veronica. He'd done pretty damned good, he thought. He could sure get used to Paige being around a little more often. Maybe they could even be exclusive fuck buddies or something. He certainly thought she was beautiful and sexy enough.

He propped himself up on an elbow watching Paige as she came out of the bathroom and gathered up her clothes. "When can we get together again?"

"Again?"

"Yeah. I mean I thought we were pretty spectacular together tonight."

"Uh. I don't know, Jacob. I mean with you livin' way out here and me in San Antonio, it might be kinda hard to get together again."

"Are you sayin' you don't want to see me after tonight?"

"No. Not really. I mean, it was good, but I can't keep coming out here indefinitely. My father is goin' to get suspicious if I keep coming home so late every weekend."

He rolled out of the bed and stalked toward her as she fastened the last button on her pants. "You're makin' excuses, Paige."

"No, really I'm—"

He wrapped his hand behind her head and crushed his mouth against hers. At first her lips were hard beneath his, but they soon softened and she opened her mouth to accept his tongue. Kissing her was like eating his favorite dessert. He wanted more, so much more. When he finally lifted his head, he whispered against her mouth, "Say I can see you again. I'm not done with this mouth."

"When?"

"I don't care. Tonight. Tomorrow. Next week. I'll take anything you'll give me."

Her fingers were splayed on his chest. The touch almost brought him to his knees. *God, I want her again.*

"I'll make something work."

"Promise?"

"Yes."

"Good girl." He swatted her butt for good measure. He loved her little squeak, which did nothing for his quickly hardening cock. She had to go. He knew that. It didn't make it any easier to watch her leave.

"Do you have a cell?"

"Of course."

"Does your dad see it?"

"No. Never."

"What's the number?"

She rattled off her cell number and he quickly memorized it to add it to his contact list. "Expect a call or text from me."

"Do I get yours?" she asked, stepping back out of his reach to slip on her boots.

"You'll have mine as soon as I send you a message." He shoved his legs into the jeans he picked up off the floor.

"True." She stood as she pressed her lips together in a firm line.

He didn't like the look at all.

"I guess I'll see you around."

"Soon."

"Yeah, soon."

She headed down the hall to the living room to retrieve her coat. "Thanks for a good time."

"You're welcome. I enjoyed myself immensely."

"Me too."

"Good."

"Good night then."

"Paige?"

"Yeah?" she asked as she turned around with her hand on the doorknob.

"Be careful going home."

Chapter Four

Paige grabbed the dandelions with her ungloved hand, yanking them from the ground surrounding the flowers in her small garden. She loved how the blooms smelled when they reached for the sun to warm their petals on this warmer than normal March afternoon. The soil between her fingers calmed her restless heart in a way she couldn't quite understand. Several flecks of dirt clung to her fingertips, coloring her pale skin to a muddy brown. The earthy smell surrounded her as the sun beat down on her bare shoulders, tingeing her fair skin to a pink, freckled slope.

A heavy sigh escaped her lips as she brushed the dirt from her hands onto her jean clad legs, smearing it along her thighs. Why couldn't she be happy with her life? Why did she have to find ways to escape her humdrum life as a preacher's daughter? The pressures of taking over the duties her mother normally would have lay heavily on her shoulders. She didn't want to be the designated woman to handle the woman's auxiliary duties or the other hundred things required of her. She wanted to be the young, careful woman of twenty-seven, live her life the way she wanted to and not have all the responsibilities of caring for the church activities.

This whole thing began after her mother was killed by a drunk driver when she was twelve. Being raised by a devote Christian preacher as a single parent left something to be desired. He'd been strict, but loving in most things, except she'd never had the love of a woman to guide her in her teen years. Now she struggled with being a woman hell-bent on proving herself as a woman. Did she pretend to be so wild so men would be attracted to her? Men liked wild women, didn't they? She wiped the sweat from her forehead smearing dirt across the bridge of her nose in the process. *Wonderful. I need a shower.*

The whole drinking until you were stinking drunk pissed her off. If the man who'd killed her mother hadn't been driving, she never would have been killed on her way home from the grocery store. Paige didn't understand how people could act so irresponsible especially at the detriment of someone else's life. She rarely drank, not liking the taste of alcohol very much and she thought people acted really stupid when they were drunk.

Her thoughts turned to Jacob as she stared at the mulch in the flower bed, spreading it with her hands to even out the lumps. She picked up a small clump, not really seeing it in her hand as she contemplated the developments between them. What the hell was she going to do with him? He seemed attracted to her at least on a physical level. They were good together in bed. She frowned. Good together in bed sounded so trite. She didn't want just a physical relationship with anyone. She wanted to get married someday, have children and build a life with a man, but then again, the physical was pretty damned good with the cowboy.

Blood hummed in her veins at the thought of the things Jacob had done to her. She'd never been so turned on in her life as she was the night they'd made love. No, had sex. Heart stopping, body humming, sex. What he'd done to her body she'd never experienced before with any man. It scared her spitless. The last thing she needed right now was another man to take care of.

She had enough troubles keeping her personal life out of her father's line of sight. Good grief! If he ever found out about where she really went on weekend nights, the poor man would probably have a heart attack or something.

Her mama would have understood.

A tear slipped down her cheek to land on the back of her hand. She quickly swiped at it with the tips of her fingers only to find more replacing them faster than she could wipe them away. Why she was crying, she wasn't sure. Just missing her mother? Maybe, but why now? Her mother had been gone over fifteen years.

"Daughter?"

"Yes, Daddy?" A very stern looking older gentleman walked down the tree-lined path toward her as she struggled to her feet, wiping at the wetness on her face and hoping he wouldn't see.

At just about six feet in height, he didn't tower over her like he used to. His green eyes were clouded with worry today as he stared down into her face. "What's wrong?"

Damn. "Nothing."

"Why are your eyes red?"

"Allergies."

"Ah."

He nodded, dismissing her emotional distress as he usually did, with the normal brush-off she found upsetting at times. Today, it didn't matter. She didn't want to explain her tears to anyone.

"Well, the ladies of the auxiliary would like to talk to you about the bake sale at the spring dance we're having as a church social."

She sighed, hating the fact that she had to take over the duties normally associated with the preacher's wife. "Yes, Daddy."

"Thank you, Paige. I know you don't always like doing these duties."

"It's not that. I just don't feel comfortable with the older ladies. There isn't anyone my age involved in these things."

"We should work on getting the younger crowd involved in the church socials. You and I should talk more about it."

"Of course."

"Wonderful. Now off you go." He kissed her on the cheek. "I'll see you at lunch."

"I love you, Daddy."

"I love you too, sweetheart."

She headed for the house to change her clothing before she went to the church. No use showing up in dirty jeans and a tank top. It wouldn't go over very well with the elderly women of the church. They already weren't too happy with the way she handled things as the daughter of the preacher.

Well too bad. She grinned as she turned on her heels to walk toward the side door of the church. It was about time they saw the true Paige.

The ladies were chattering like squirrels on the hunt for nuts. None paid much attention to Paige as she came to stand behind them.

"Really. She's such a nice girl, but she just doesn't have it in her to be a preacher's daughter."

Oh hell no!

One of the ladies looked past Mrs. Johnson and swallowed visibly. Paige shook her head as she pressed her fingers to her lips.

Another of the threesome said, "And the Preacher Tyler is such a great man. He's so personable and handsome. Oh, lordy is he handsome."

Paige almost giggled. Obviously the widow Martin had the hots for her father.

"Well of course he is, but he's still very distraught over his wife's death."

"But she died over fifteen years ago."

"Apparently he isn't ready to move on."

"I think I might invite him and Paige over for Sunday dinner this week. You know, to be neighborly and all."

"Of course."

"Where is that girl anyway?" Mrs. Johnson spun around. "Paige?"

"Mrs. Johnson. Widow Martin. Mrs. Williams. Nice to see you ladies."

All three women took in her attire and frowned. "Gardening?" Mrs. Johnson asked.

"Yes, I was. It's a beautiful spring day out there. The sun is just warm enough and the flowers are blooming. My daffodils are budding and they look so pretty next to the ground cover blooms that are starting to come up as well. My Agarita are out now too."

"You have a beautiful garden, Paige," Mrs. Williams choked out, obviously embarrassed by the talk going on around her while Paige listened.

"Thank you. I do love gardening." She stuffed her hands in her pockets. "Shall we get down to business so I can get back to it?"

“Certainly.”

For the next hour the four women chatted, drank tea and made notes about the spring social event the church was planning. They were going to have a carnival type atmosphere with a dance later in the evening to bring in the local younger crowd.

“And with the dance, we should be able to draw some of the locals in, I would think,” Widow Martin said.

“What kind of music are they listenin’ to these days, Paige?”

“This area would be great for a country music type dance I would think. Maybe bring in a local band. I know someone—”

“Oh no.” Mrs. Johnson shook her head with enough force her glasses tilted. “We couldn’t have a band.”

“Why not? I think it’s a great idea.”

“Bands tend to bring in the drinkers. You know. The kind of people who hang out in those seedy bars.”

Seedy bars? The Dusty Boot wasn’t a seedy bar. The ladies would fall over dead if they saw her in her leather gear or saw the tall drink of water wrapped up in the package of Jacob Young.

Her nipples pebbled at the mere thought of the man.

“Cold dear?” Widow Martin asked with a raised eyebrow and a glance at her chest.

“Uh, yeah.”

“You should have worn a sweater. It’s not quite warm enough for those skimpy tops you young girl’s wear these days.”

“I’m fine.” She crossed her arms over her chest and scowled. “Back to the band? If we want to draw in the younger crowd, we need to have something they'll like in order to get them into the festivities. Punch and cookies aren't going to do it. I'm not suggesting alcohol be served, but a band would be great."

"Well I think it's a good idea."

The deep voice behind her made her jump as she swung around. "I thought you were leaving this to us women, Daddy?"

"I was." He nodded to the other women as he placed a hand on her shoulder. "I thought I would put in my two cents. I think having a band come and play during the party is a grand idea." He tipped his head to the side as heat crawled up her neck. "How on earth do you know anyone in a band, Paige?"

"I, *uh…*"

"Never mind. I'm sure it's one of your friends who mentioned it or something. If you know someone who might be interested in playing, by all means, talk to them."

"Are you sure?"

"Of course. Maybe we should have this over the Memorial Day holiday? Wouldn't it be grand to have a barbeque picnic type thing with a band, fireworks, and games?"

"What a wonderful idea, Reverend Tyler," Widow Martin interjected. "You come up with such fantastic ideas."

The older woman batted her eyelashes as Paige shook her head and rolled her eyes.

"Thank you. Anyway, I'll let you ladies work out the details. We have a few months to plan this if we are doing it over Memorial Day weekend. You'll need to work on this to get it planned." He rubbed his hands together. "This will be wonderful to bring in the local community as well as some of the younger crowd."

Her father smiled as he walked toward the back of the church with a new spring in his step. Paige hadn't seen him this excited about something in a long time. Maybe this would be good for all of them.

Talk switched to the Memorial Day celebration as they were now calling it. Paige took over the job of booking a band. She had the perfect one in mind if they would do it, the band from The Dusty Boot. Of course, it depended on whether they were available or not. If not, they might know someone who would fit the bill.

She tapped her fingers against her lips. Would some of the families from Bandera come? What about inviting Jacob and his family? They probably didn't go to church in San Antonio, but it might be a chance to see him outside of their once a week hookup from The Dusty Boot.

"Paige?"

"Oh. Sorry. My mind wandered there for a minute. Did you have a question?"

"You never did answer us or your father. Where do you know a country music band from?" Mrs. Johnson asked.

"Oh around. I have a couple of friends who sing in a band."

"Not the type of people I would think a preacher's daughter should be hanging around with," the widow said with a frown.

"Sorry, ladies. It's time for me to leave. I must get lunch on the table for my father." She stood. "We'll talk again soon. In the meantime, I'll be looking into the band." Paige quickly dismissed herself from the company of the women to avoid talking about her personal life. They didn't need to know anything about her, the busybodies. Her life was her own to live and damn it, live it she would.

The cooler interior of the small house she and her father shared greeted her with warmth. She loved living there even though it held some hard memories of her mother. The church had welcomed them into the family many years ago, but it was time for them to let her lead her life in whatever manner she chose.

"Daddy?"

"In here, sweetheart," her father called from the small den.

She headed down the little hall until she approached the doorway leading into her father's office. "Are you ready for lunch?"

"Sure, honey." He never glanced up from his laptop.

She sighed in disappointment. On one hand she wished he would take more of an interest in what her life held, but on the other hand she hoped he'd never know about the more intimate details.

After a moment, she turned and headed to the kitchen. Sandwiches and chips would have to do. She hadn't been to the grocery for their weekly staples. She quickly made their lunch and delivered it to her father's desk, knowing he wouldn't join her at the table. The solitary life they led drove her crazy. She needed to be around people on a regular basis. *Might as well do the grocery shopping now.*

She finished her lunch and went to her room to change her clothes. Even though she didn't mind being seen with dirty jeans and a smudge of mud across her nose, her father would be appalled if she went out in public in her gardening attire. With a bright sundress hugging her curves, she slipped on a pair of sandals and grabbed her purse. She stopped at the mirror in the hall to wipe the dirt from her nose as she called, “I’m going to the store, Daddy. I’ll be back in a little while.”

He still never looked up as she glanced through the doorway. “Be careful, sweetheart.”

“I will.”

“Don’t forget to stop at the liquor store. My bottle is empty.”

It had been half full last week. “Of course.” At least he only drank at home.

Once outside the house, she slid into her car and shut the door. This little excursion would give her some time away. She loved her father, but he did get on her nerves once in a while. Probably more often than she cared to admit sometimes. “Maybe if he started dating again, he wouldn’t be so worried about my life.”

The grocery store came into a view a few minutes later. It really was more of a large food outlet than a grocery store, but when she did their major shopping, she liked the warehouse bargains of the store.

The place was mobbed. Why there were so many people there was beyond her. *Oh yeah, it’s Saturday. Oh hell.* She found a parking spot next to a large, crew cab truck and stepped out. The swarm of people heading for the doors felt almost suffocating, but she managed to go with the flow and reach the front.

One cart left. She grabbed it, flashed her card at the door attendant and went inside. The cooler air of the store felt good on her skin. With the list in her hand she'd grabbed from the refrigerator door at home, she moved down the first aisle. Laundry soap, dryer sheets, starch for her father's collars. Slowly her cart filled until she reached the meat section. She found the steaks, chicken and ribs she'd been looking for until a beautiful dark haired woman next to her glanced over. The woman had the most beautiful dark brown eyes she'd ever seen.

"Those ribs looks fantastic, don't they?" the woman said as she grabbed a package to put in her cart.

"I love the meat here. They always have such a wonderful selection and quality. Do you shop here all the time?"

"Yes. We have a lot of people we cook for." Paige glanced at the woman's cart piled high with meat. "This will only last us about a week."

"Wow."

"We run a guest ranch so we have to feed a lot of people."

"Oh, how fun. I bet you have a great place."

"We try. We run cattle too, but it's mostly the guests these days and my boys. They'll eat me out of this food quickly enough."

Boys?

"I have nine of them and two wonderful new daughters-in-law. Oh, and a wonderful grandson and another on the way."

"I love big families."

"We definitely have one of those."

As she looked down at the package of meat in her hands, Paige blanched as a deep voice penetrated her conscious thought. "Well hi, Paige."

Oh shit. It can't be! She turned to her left only to look up into the brown-eyed gaze of Jacob.

* * * *

The last person he expected to see at the store when his mother suggested he accompany her was Paige. Not that he hadn't thought a lot about her over the last several weeks. If truth be told, he'd thought of little else except her pebbled nipples in those clamps or of her pussy slick with juice and ready for him as he slid home.

"What are you doin' here?"

"Shopping."

"I see. Oh, Mom this is Paige. Paige this is my mother, Nina."

"It's nice to meet you, Paige. How do you know Jacob?"

"We met a few weeks ago," she said in a choked up voice as she threw the meat in her cart.

"At The Dusty Boot," Jacob added.

Nina's eyebrows rose as she did a double take at Paige. "I see."

"No, really you don't. I don't frequent bars." Paige started to breathe faster, her chest rising and falling rapidly. Panic flashed in her eyes.

"It's fine. I understand perfectly."

"I, *uh*, have to go."

"Wait."

"No. I really need to go. My father is waiting for me in another aisle."

"Great. I'd love to meet him."

"No!" She grabbed her cart and disappeared around the edge of the aisle.

"Paige!" Jacob rounded the corner, walking quickly to catch up with her. "Wait."

"Leave me alone, Jacob."

"Why?" He grabbed her arm, pulling her to a stop. "What's wrong?" He glanced around, but there weren't any other patrons in the paper goods aisle. Surrounded by toilet paper, paper towels and napkins, he tried to soothe her with a calming hand on her arm.

"I don't want to get involved with you on a personal level, Jacob. We had sex. That's it." The alarm in her gaze hadn't dissipated.

Disappointment rushed through him. He wanted more from her although he wasn't sure how much more. *Keep it simple.* "But you never answered my text or my calls."

"Maybe I needed some room to breathe."

"I don't want you to feel suffocated. I'm sorry if bein' with me does that to you."

"It's not that." She shook off his hold. "I need some space. Meeting your family is too much."

"I'm sorry. It just happened. Not that I could have controlled when you met my family by running into us at the store."

She swallowed visibly as she pressed her hand to her chest. "I'm sorry for losing it. I just never expected to see you anywhere other than the bar, I guess."

"I like the dress."

"Thanks."

"You look beautiful."

"Stop, Jacob. Just stop, okay?"

"What am I doin' wrong here, Paige? I thought women liked bein' complimented on their looks."

She took a step back. "I need to go."

"Can we get together again this weekend?"

"I don't know. Don't press me."

"All right fine." He pushed his fingers through his hair. *Women!* "How about you call me when you want a little action since bein' nice doesn't seem to get through to you. If you want rough and tumble, baby, you got it." He grabbed the back of her head so he could press his mouth against hers. The pressure of his kiss didn't lessen even when her lips softened under his. When he finally let her go, her lips were swollen and red. "See you around, darlin'."

Chapter Five

Memorial Day weekend. Paige shuddered with concern, she didn't want this weekend to happen at all, but here it was. She dreaded the days with every passing month since March, since the last time she'd seen Jacob. He hadn't called. No text. Nothing. Her dreams were haunted with his touch. She woke many a morning trembling with need and hungry for his kiss, but she refused to reach out to him.

"Are you sure everything is ready, Paige."

"Yes, Daddy. It'll be a great party. The band is set to be here by seven and will play until ten. All the games are ready. The fireworks will be handled by the pyrotechnic company. Don't worry."

"I want this to be a wholesome celebration to bring the younger crowd to our church."

"Do you have your sermon ready?"

"Yes."

"Can I read it?"

"Of course."

He handed her the paper. She scanned the wording, cringing at a few lines here and there, but overall, it wasn't bad. "I think it's fine. You are planning on having the sermon this morning at eleven and then the barbeque will start, correct?"

"Yes. Our regular church members will be there, I'm sure. I'm hoping new members will come for church services before the barbeque starts."

Paige glanced down at her sundress. The bright red complimented her skin without making it too sallow like it usually did. Of course, it helped that she'd been gardening a lot the last several weeks while she avoided indulging in her secret life. Her restless soul screamed for release from her humdrum existence, but she refused to give in for fear of seeing Jacob. She didn't know whether she could handle being close to him without dropping to her knees so he would fuck her silly.

The weather had warmed up considerably for the end of May as it was prone to do in Texas. The sun beat down relentlessly as she set up the table for the punch. Luckily, most of the food and drinks were under tents the church had rented, although the sermon would be outside. She hoped the temperature wouldn't climb too high today.

The church bell clanged signaling the beginning of festivities as people began pouring onto the grounds behind the church. She smiled as the crowd grew with young and old. Hope sprang in her heart for some younger members who would be willing to start attending their church, for her father's sake, of course. It would be nice to have a few others to hang with and talk to during bible studies.

She glanced across the lawn in time to see a large family group walking toward one of the big trees. All of the men wore cowboy hats and the three women with them wore shorts or sundresses. Her heart skipped a beat when she noticed one of the women was extremely pregnant and another had beautiful long, black hair tied back in a braid. A small boy ran around in circles until one of the cowboys picked him up to swing him up on his shoulders.

It couldn't be.

One tall cowboy peeled away from the group once they were all settled and headed toward her. *Shit. No, no, no.* She quickly looked to her left and right trying to figure out where to hide. The last thing she wanted at this party was to run into him. *What the hell is he doin' here.* She spun to her right and disappeared out of the tent headed for the house. Surely he wouldn't follow her there.

Wrong.

The moment she opened the door, she heard the clomp of his boots on the wooden porch of the house.

"Paige."

"Jacob." Her breath came in shallow gulps of air as she tried to get her rapid heart under control.

"Why are you runnin', darlin'?"

"What are you doing here?"

"My family heard about the party for the weekend and thought it would be a great way to get to know some people in San Antonio. Besides, it has been awhile. I thought you might've been a little lonely."

She turned to face him. "You knew this was my father's church?"

"I had your phone number, remember? It's not hard to get information once you have that."

"You asswipe!"

"Tsk, tsk. Such language from a daughter of God."

She pulled back her hand, landing a stinging slap to his left cheek. "Fuck you, Jacob! How dare you use this as an opportunity to corner me." When she moved to do it again, he grabbed her hand and slowly reeled her in like a fish on a hook.

"You got one. Don't push it." He walked her backward into the house and slammed the door behind them. "Miss me?"

"Not in this lifetime." The warmth of his breath on her mouth had her lips tingling for the touch of his. Had she missed him? Damn right, she had. More than she'd ever let onto him. To hell with him! He hadn't called or anything, the bastard. *Not like I tried to call him either.*

"Oh, I bet you did, baby." He nibbled at the corners of her mouth. "I missed you."

The slow glide of the tip of his tongue over her bottom lip had her trapping a moan in her throat as her eyes drifted shut. Her lips parted as she swiped her tongue over her lips hoping to brush it with his.

The palm of his hand abraded her nipple through her dress, forcing the groan to the surface of her mouth.

His mouth slid along her jaw to her ear, the scrape of his whiskers sending her body into an overdrive of sensation. Goose bumps skittered across the flesh of her arms when his breath tickled the whorl. He nipped at her earlobe as she tipped her head to the side asking, no begging for more.

"Paige?"

"Shit. It's my father coming in the back door," she growled, pushing against his chest with her hands. "Let go!"

Jacob stepped back as she smoothed her dress down and turned to face her father as he came in through the doorway from the kitchen into the living room. "In here, Daddy. I was checking to make sure I didn't forget anything."

"Oh. Well, hello there." He held out his hand. "I'm Paige's father, Reverend Tyler."

"It's nice to meet you, sir." Jacob shook her father's hand. "I'm Jacob Young. My family is here for the picnic. We have a place out in Bandera."

"Wonderful! I'm thrilled to see some young people here." He turned to face her. "Isn't this wonderful, Paige? It's what we hoped for."

Jacob faced her as well and she wanted to punch the smug look off his face. "Yes, Daddy. It's great. I'm sure it'll be lots of fun."

"How do you two know each other? I'm surprised I haven't met you before, young man."

"We met at—"

"The nursing home, Daddy. He has a family member who is a resident there."

Jacob's eyebrow rose as a smirk settled on his mouth. "That's right. At the nursing home."

"Do you volunteer there as well?"

"Not as much as I used to, sir. I don't get there very often these days."

"That's too bad."

"Yes, yes it is, but I'm a better person now and I felt my time there needed to be more limited so I could spend it helping my family at home on our ranch."

"You own a ranch?"

"My family does, yes. It's a guest ranch, but we also run cattle."

"How fascinating. A real cowboy."

"To the bone, sir."

"I think we have everything. Why don't we head back out to greet our guests, Daddy? I'm sure everyone will be wondering where we are." She glanced at her watch. "It's about time for the games to begin anyway."

"Of course, Paige." He hugged her to his side as a wide grin spread across his mouth. "I'm so proud of you for organizing this."

"You organized the party? Wow."

"Not all of it. I was on the committee."

"We're having a live band later."

"Awesome. Save me a dance?" Jacob asked with the same silly smirk on his face. The bastard. He knew she wouldn't say no in front of her father.

"Of course, Jacob, but I think it's time to join the others." She peeled herself away from her father and headed for the door. The only way she was going to get them back outside as they stood there chatting, was to push them out.

The two men followed her back outside into the bright sunshine toward the food tent. She wanted to check on things again, plus she needed to put some distance between her and Jacob. It drove her nuts to think of how easily she succumbed to his advances in the house. She'd practically melted into a puddle of goo at his feet from merely the brush of his mouth on her skin. That wouldn't do. Never mind how his hand felt on her breast, kneading the globe with his palm and pinching her nipple between his fingers hard enough to remind her of the nipple clamps.

"Would you like something to drink, Jacob?" she asked, politeness dripping from her words like honey from the comb.

"I would love some, but let me check on the family to see if they need anything." He disappeared back toward the group by the tree as her father watched him walk away.

"What a nice young man."

"*Uh*, yeah."

"Now, he's the kind of man you should be looking for, Paige. Charming, well-mannered, and I bet he's a good Christian man."

Paige spit the water she'd just taken into her mouth out, in a spray of liquid. Luckily, she didn't get anyone with it. "Don't get ahead of yourself, Daddy. I haven't known Jacob that long. We only met a few months ago."

"Well, your mother and I didn't know each other long either before I knew she was the love of my life."

"I know you loved Mom with your whole heart, but you probably should think about dating again."

"Pah! I don't need to date. I have you to do the duties for me so why should I look for another woman?"

"Someday, I'll move out and have a family of my own. I won't be here to do everything like I am now."

"I know, Paige, but it'll be a few years yet I'm hoping. Besides, the woman's auxiliary can handle most of those things with or without you."

"Then why do you insist I do them? I could be out with my friends, finding a husband, raising a family." She stomped her foot. "I hate doing all of these things."

"Paige." He glanced around them noting the few stares she was sure were aimed their way now. "We can discuss this another time."

"Fine," she grumbled. "This conversation isn't over by a long shot."

She whirled around and almost ran nose first into Jacob's chin. "Let's walk, shall we," he said, taking her arm in his firm grasp.

"Fine."

He tucked her hand into the crook of his arm and headed down the knoll toward the cemetery. "Is your Mom here?"

"Yes." They ducked under a tree branch. "To the back on the left."

They wandered in that direction, stopping to note some of the smaller stones as she often wondered what the story was of the souls lost so long ago. The church had been there for over a hundred years and there were several families buried in the cemetery, some from the late 1800's.

Tears gathered in her eyes as she got closer and closer to her mother's headstone. She silently wiped at the tears with her fingertips, hoping Jacob wouldn't see.

"Sshh." He turned her in his arms and held her to his chest.

Broken sobs tore at her throat as she cried into his neck, soaking his shirt. He never asked any questions, just held her tight, all the time sweeping his hand over her braid.

After several minutes she stepped back. He wiped the remaining tears from her cheeks with his thumbs.

"Seems you've needed a good cry for a while."

"I guess I did. Thank you."

"No thanks needed, darlin'."

She swallowed hard. The endearment from his lips almost made her forget the animosity between them. She wanted to forget the loneliness of the last two months without him. "Just hold me."

"My pleasure, baby."

They stood in the silence of the grounds with the laughter of the fair atmosphere in the distance, for some time. The warmth emanating from his skin as he rubbed his hands up and down her back, made her want to sink into him and never come out. "I suppose we should get back. Your family will be worried about you."

"It's fine. Mom knew I was headed your direction."

"Well my father will be worried. I was supposed to announce the games."

"I think Charlie from the band took over for you. I hear his deep baritone announcing away." They turned to walk back toward the crowd with their arms around each other.

"You didn't want to participate?"

"Only if there are three legged races and you are my partner." He stopped to kiss her nose. "Are you okay?"

"Yeah, I'm fine. Again, thank you for the shoulder."

"I have some pretty broad ones so anytime you need one, you holler."

"I could do that." She reached up and kissed the corner of his mouth. With his hand in hers, they walked back into the refreshment tent so she could take over some of the duties from the other ladies of the auxiliary.

Jacob smiled for a minute, tipped his hat and wandered back to his family.

His family. Next he would want to introduce her to everyone. She wasn't sure she was ready for that kind of familiarity. Well hell, he'd met her father even though it wasn't planned on her part. *I guess it wouldn't hurt to meet his family.*

She could pretend it was on the pretense of inviting them all to the potato sack races going on in a few minutes. *Sure, what a plan!* She shook her head as she told one of the teenage girls helping her she would be right back.

The entire clan size overwhelmed her a little when she made her way closer, but the warmth in Jacob's eyes as she walked toward him, dissipated all the butterflies in her stomach.

"Well hello. Paige, isn't it?" Nina asked when she stopped next to the group.

They all looked her way as she blushed bright red. "Yes, ma'am. It's nice to see you again."

"You too."

"I wanted to invite everyone to enjoy the games we are having. I believe the potato sack races are next."

Jacob touched her elbow, drawing her attention back to his family. "Let me introduce you to the group, Paige. These are my parents. You know Nina, my mother and sitting next to her is James, my father."

"Ma'am."

"Nice to meet you."

"These are my brothers, Jeff and his girl Terri." He indicated with a nod to one couple next to the tree in the shade.

"Nice to meet you."

"My other brothers, Jason, Joshua, Jackson, Joey, Jeremiah and Jonathan." He pointed to another couple to the right of the huge blanket. "And over there is Joel and Mesa."

"Wow, what a group."

All of the men tipped their hats and grinned while the women smiled and waved. "The little rascal running around is Jeff's son Ben."

The announcer shouted about the potato sack races as four of the brothers jumped to their feet.

"Can I get anyone anything to drink? There is soda, water, coffee and ice tea at the refreshment tent. From the smells coming from the barbeque area I would say the food will be ready soon."

"Great! I'm starved," Joshua said, whisking by her on his way to grab a sack.

She watched him as she laughed at the exuberance of the group. Typical men.

Jacob's hand dropped to her hip in an almost possessive way, which she found kind of endearing around his brothers. Did he want to stake a claim on her around his bachelor brothers? She put her hand on top of his to remove it, but he held firm. He wasn't budging as his fingers dug into her hip.

"I think we're fine, Paige, but thank you," Nina said. "Unless Terri or Mesa need something?"

"I'm fine, Mom," Mesa said as she jumped to her feet. "I'm going to go beat the pants off these Young brothers in the potato sack races."

"Terri," Jeff asked, smoothing his hand over her protruding belly. "Do you need somethin', honey?"

"I'm fine too. I have my water."

"Just don't overdo. Let me know when you want to go home."

"Yes, Dad." She kissed him on the mouth. "I'm fine. Stop worrying."

Paige thought it was cute how the men took care of their women. She wanted that someday, but could Jacob be man enough to treat her like something precious in his life? Maybe. She didn't want to be treated like an antique piece of furniture to be admired, but never handled. She needed a man's touch, his touch.

He'd been so loving out at the cemetery when she'd busted out in blubbering tears all over his shirt. She really began to wonder if the Jacob who had been seemed cut off from everything two months ago, really existed.

"Well, it was great meeting you all. Let me know if you need anything. Enjoy the festivities."

"It was great meeting you, Paige. Come back and visit when you have a moment," Nina said with a smile.

"I will." She turned out of Jacob's hold. "I have to get back."

"I'll walk back with you."

"It's okay."

"I want to."

She sighed as she rolled her eyes.

"I saw that."

A giggle escaped her lips the minute he spun her around to face him and pressed his lips to hers.

Her hands pressed against his chest as he lifted his mouth. The deep brown of his eyes twinkled in the sunlight, letting her know he'd kissed her on purpose to let everyone in the area know they were a couple. *But we aren't, are we?*

"Yes, we are," he said, pecking her on the lips again before he wrapped an arm around her waist to escort her to the tent.

"Did I say that out loud?"

"Yeah, you did and I did it for that reason. Everyone around now knows we are together."

Chapter Six

The afternoon had been wonderful. Jacob was attentive and sweet. They'd even won the three-legged race by him practically carrying her down the race course. But when they'd fallen at the end, she'd ended up on top of him. Her body went haywire as his scent and touch surrounded her. Every muscle bunched beneath her, reminding her of how he'd fucked her senseless. She wanted that again more than anything in this world.

Now she stood wrapped in his arms as the band played a slow song. They swayed to the music as if they were meant to dance together for a lifetime. It scared the shit out of her.

"I shouldn't be dancing with you."

"Why not," he whispered, his lips pressed to her ear.

"Because I'm hosting this shindig. I should be working."

"You can have fun too."

"I shouldn't be."

"Yes you should. You did a fabulous job with this party. Tons of people came. Your father's little church is on the map now."

"I wonder how many people will come to services."

"I think a lot will. I overheard several people talking about how personable your father is and how they would love to attend his sermons."

"What about the younger people? We need a new crowd to keep the church going."

"My family has been looking for a church to attend. The one they were going to before, the pastor left. They don't like the new one."

"I'm sure with a prominent family like yours attending, we'll get a great turn out."

"You might have to build a bigger church."

She glanced up as surprise raced through her. "We love this little church. It's been here for over a hundred years. We don't want a bigger, fancier one."

"What if the congregation grows so big, you can't handle it in this church? I mean a big wedding would be hard pressed to attend in there. It's quaint, yes, but it's very small."

"But it's beautiful. My mother used to sing in the choir in there. My father has been preaching there for over fifteen years. They can't want a bigger church."

"Easy, darlin'. It's just a thought."

"Well, get that thought right out of your head, Jacob. I won't have them tearing down my church."

"No one said anything about tearing it down."

"But they would have to so they could build a bigger one. Bigger isn't always better."

"Honey, calm down."

"I won't! No one is tearing down this church."

Jacob pressed his lips to hers as she twisted in his arms. How could he want to kiss her while she was so upset?

Her mind sidetracked to the feel of his lips on hers. She loved to have him kiss her. Her mouth opened to the touch of his tongue as she wrapped her arms around his neck.

A moment later, a throat clearing penetrated her foggy brain. She glanced over Jacob's shoulder to see the frown on her father's face. *Oops.*

"Hi."

"Can I speak to you a minute, Paige?"

"Sure." She gave Jacob a peck on the mouth figuring she was already in deep shit, what did one more kiss hurt. She followed her father into the shadows, prepared for the reprimand coming.

"Paige, is it necessary to be kissing the man like that in front of everyone? Where are your morals, young lady?"

"Right where they should be, Daddy."

"I find your behavior offensive and I won't have you pawing at him in front of parishioners. You're acting like some loose woman."

"Maybe I am. There is nothing wrong with me."

"I didn't say there was, Paige, but this behavior isn't becoming of you in the least. You don't act like this. What would your mother think?"

"I have to believe mother would be happy for me." She closed her eyes for a moment, but when she reopened them, the disappointment in his eyes still hurt her heart. "I'm sorry you are upset with me over this, but I like Jacob. A lot. You said yourself he seemed like a nice Christian man when you met him earlier."

"That was before I saw him seducing my daughter in front of the churchgoers."

"He wasn't seducing me. He kissed me. Nothing more."

"With tongues!"

"Like you never kissed mother with your tongue."

"We were married."

"So maybe I'm marrying Jacob!"

"Whoa." Jacob stepped into the shadows. "We aren't gettin' married."

"I know that!"

"Then don't say we are."

"Just stop, all right. It's nothing, Father. We weren't having sex in the middle of the dance floor."

"You might as well have been."

"Really? What we were doing wasn't even close to what sex was like between us."

"Paige!" Both her father and Jacob yelled at the same time.

"What? It's wasn't and you know it to be true, Jacob. What happened between us was a lot more explosive than merely kissing out there."

"You've had sex with him?" Her father whipped his finger between the two of them. "The two of you had sex?"

"Yes, Daddy we did. Not that big of a deal."

"Oh my." Her father stepped aside, sinking onto a chair sitting near the empty refreshment tent flap. "Heavenly Father, please help this wayward child come back to your loving presence. Show her that premarital sex isn't the right thing to do and that you forgive her for her sins."

"I'm sorry, but I don't think there is anything wrong with it."

"Now Paige," Jacob added.

"Don't now Paige me, buddy." She pressed her finger into the middle of his chest. "You were there too so you've done your sinly duties in this mess too."

"Ask for forgiveness, Paige, and the Lord will see you've repented."

"I'm not, Daddy. What I had with Jacob was wonderful and I'm not sorry."

"Go to the house then."

"No."

"Paige—"

"I'm not twelve anymore, Father. So stop treating me like I am. I'm a grown woman. If I want to have sex with Jacob, I will. If I want to stay out late, I will. If I don't want to go the nursing home anymore, I will." She dropped to her knees in front of him as she took his hands in hers. "I'm twenty-seven years old, Daddy. I can make my own decisions."

He swept her bangs away from her face. "When did you grow up?"

"A long time ago."

"I never saw it coming. I want my little girl back."

"She's still inside me, Daddy, but she only comes out to enjoy sunshine picnics, swing sets and daydreams." She kissed his cheek. "I have my own life to lead now. I can't be what you want me to be." She stood and walked into Jacob's arms. "Let's go watch the fireworks."

Her father stayed on the chair as she led Jacob down to the knoll where they could see the fireworks better.

"You didn't have to do that, you know."

"Yes, I did. I needed him to see me for the real me instead of the child he remembers me as."

"You broke his heart."

"I don't think so, but I do wish my mother were here. She would understand and help him understand." Jacob sat on the grass and pulled her between his legs so her buttocks rested against his crotch. "Happy to see me, big boy?"

"Always, baby. It's been a while."

"For you too? I wondered."

"I haven't been with anyone since we were together, Paige."

"Why?"

"Because I wanted you."

"Sounds like a serious ailment."

"It is. It's been torture the last two months. I haven't masturbated that many times since I turned fifteen."

The band quit playing as the fireworks started exploding over their heads with the appropriate *ohs* and *ahs* from the crowd with each burst of color. Jacob's hands did a slow crawl up and down her arms as she snuggled against his chest with her back.

"You look beautiful today."

"Thank you."

"It's kind of strange seeing you without your leather."

"You saw me at the store without it."

"Yeah, but I was surprised." He played with her braid. "I like your hair loose better so I can run my fingers through the strands."

"I didn't want it loose so it was in the food or anything."

"It's soft." He tickled her cheek with the end of her braid. "I love it wrapped around my fist as I fuck you senseless."

"Charmer."

"I can't wait to get you alone."

"It might be a bit. I have to clean up."

“I’ll help.” He wrapped his arms around her waist as she settled hers on top of his. “I love holding you like this.”

“We didn’t do any snuggling really, when we were together before.”

“We haven’t done a lot of things dating couples do.”

“Are we dating?”

“What do you think?”

She sighed.

“That didn’t sound very happy.”

“I am. I’m just upset with my father. The conversation didn’t go well.”

“Let’s get this talk about us out of the way first and then we’ll worry about your father. Okay?”

“Sure. What do you want to talk about?”

“We’re dating, right?”

“I guess. I mean you haven’t really asked me out or anything. You just show up here, bully-kiss me and then expect to be welcomed with open arms.”

“Yep. That’s about it.”

“Typical man.”

“No. A man who knows what he wants and got tired of waiting for the woman to figure it out. You didn’t call me.”

“No, I didn’t.” She plucked at the hair on his arm, pulling slightly. “Not that I didn’t think about you, *a hell of a lot.*”

“I’m glad I wasn’t alone then, because I thought about you a lot too.”

“You don’t know how many times I pick up the phone to call, but lost my nerve.”

“Why?” he asked, concern in his voice.

"I wasn't sure what to say to you," she whispered, unsure of confessing all her secrets to him would be a wise decision.

"How about I want to see you?"

She shook her head. "Too easy. I knew I wanted to see you, but it would have meant an apology for my erratic behavior at the store."

"Why did you freak?"

She shifted so she could look into his eyes. "We'd slept together once, Jacob, and there you were introducing me to your mother."

"It wasn't a big deal, Paige. It was only a coincidence thing. Not something I planned. It wasn't like a big family to-do where you came over to the house so everyone could meet you because we were getting married or something."

"I know, but meeting the family seems too permanent to me."

"You met everyone today."

"Yeah, but you realize it was after you met my father."

"Which we hadn't planned either." He stroked a finger down her cheek. "He wasn't at the store was he?"

"No. It was an excuse to leave."

"I figured as much."

"I'm sorry I lied."

"Don't lie to me again or I'll punish you."

"Punish me?"

"Remember your spanking before?"

"Yeah and I didn't like it."

"You wouldn't like it if I gave you another one, would you?"

"No." She bit her lip for a moment. "I thought there was more to doing kinky things than smacking on a person."

"Oh, there is and smacking on a person isn't the same."

"I won't allow you to beat on me."

"I don't beat on women."

"What do you call the spanking then?"

"I wasn't beating on you. I was letting you know who is in charge of this relationship."

"We aren't in a relationship and we certainly weren't then."

"What would you call this then?"

"I don't know."

"Dating is a sort of relationship."

"I guess so."

"You don't want a relationship with me?"

"It's not that. I didn't think you wanted anything permanent. Eventually, I want a husband, family, two point five kids, and a white picket fence. You don't seem into those things."

"Maybe not right now, but I might be in the future."

"Are you helping us clean up, Paige?" Mrs. Johnson asked, stopping next to where they sat on the ground.

"Yes, ma'am. We'll be right there."

Mrs. Johnson walked toward the refreshment tent as Paige climbed to her feet. She held out her hand to help Jacob up, which he kissed her palm, ran his tongue around her first finger, and then jumped to his feet.

"Come on, doll. Let's get this cleaned up so we can get some alone time."

"Such a charmer you are, Mr. Young."

"I aim to please, darlin'." He tucked his arm around her waist and escorted her to the refreshment tent.

Several minutes later, his entire family arrived to help clean up as well.

"We're here to help," Jeremiah said, standing next to the table. "Tell us what you want us to do."

As she directed everyone, she smiled. Why wasn't she surprised that his family would jump in and help with the cleanup even though it was getting late in the evening.

"Paige, it was nice to meet you. We would stay to help, but I need to get Terri and Ben home," Jeff said, holding out his hand.

"Oh, it's fine. Thank you for coming. We hope to see you all in church someday soon."

"We will. Give us a couple of weeks. Terri is about to pop and I don't want her to be doing too much right now."

"Oh stop it, Jeff. I'm not the first woman to have a baby. Besides, we still have a few months to go."

"But you are havin' my baby, honey. I take care of you."

"Yes you do and I love you for it." She kissed him on the lips as she snuggled closer to his side. "Thank you for inviting us to the barbeque. It was fabulous."

"You're very welcome."

"Jacob, Mom. We'll see y'all at home."

"Be careful driving home, Jeff."

"We will. Night all."

She watched Jeff, Terri and a sleepy Ben walk toward the parked cars hoping someday to have what they had. The next thing to catch her eye was

Joel and Mesa. They stacked chairs together in one corner as he snuck a kiss with each chair they put on the stack. *Wow. They seem so in love.*

"What's the sigh for, darlin'?"

"I love watching your family. Those paired off seem like they love each other so much."

He slipped his arm around her waist as he brushed a warm kiss across her cheek. "Yeah, they do. I'm glad my brothers found it in each of the women they have. I wondered about Jeff for a long time. He had it pretty rough with Ben's momma."

"Oh?"

"Yeah. I won't bore you with the details right now, but lucky for him she's no longer in the picture."

"I can't imagine anyone leaving their child."

"She overdosed late last year on meth."

"Wow."

"Things were pretty messed up with her. I'll tell you about it some other time. We're almost done with this clean up so we can get out of here."

"I think we're done. The tent guys will be here tomorrow to tear down the tents. We just need to move the chairs to the back so they'll be able to load them easier, fold up the tables, and put the coolers with the leftover drinks at the rear of the church."

Jacob whistled to get his brothers attention. Once he gave them all directions on what needed to be done and moved, things went smoothly until all was accomplished.

"Nice to have such wonderful help," Mrs. Johnson said stopping near where they stood.

"Yes, it is." Paige surveyed the area to make sure everything was in its place.

“How do you know them?”

“Paige and I are dating,” Jacob replied, kissing her on the cheek.

“I didn’t know you had a boyfriend, Paige.” She leaned in to whisper, “He’s quite handsome too.”

“I think so.”

Jacob threw back his head and roared with laughter. “I think I like her.”

Mrs. Johnson blushed as she excused herself, grabbed her purse, and headed for her car.

Once the crowd had dispersed, she grabbed the front of Jacob’s shirt to pull him in for a kiss. Shadows surrounded them, shifting with each movement of the trees overhead. Moonlight bled through the leaves, scattering silver beams across the ground. She didn’t see her father standing in the shadows until he cleared his throat in the midst of their kiss.

A sigh escaped her lips as she turned to face her father. “Daddy.”

“Paige, can we talk?” he asked in a timid voice, one she’d never heard him use before.

Not wanting to give up her time with Jacob, she said, “Not now. We’re done cleaning up, but I’m going out with Jacob for a while. Don’t wait up.”

“But—”

“I’m sorry, Daddy. We’ll talk tomorrow.”

“All right.” She heard the disappointment as he disappeared into the shadows surrounding the side of the church.

Several moments later, she heard the door to their little house close.

“You really should have talked to him.”

"I can't. Not tonight. I'm still upset with him and his irrational behavior."

"He wasn't being irrational, Paige. He's trying to protect you."

"I don't need protecting, remember?"

"I know you can take care of yourself physically in a fight, but darlin', he is your father. He wants what is best for you."

She brushed her lips against his. "Can we not talk about this right now?" She plucked at the buttons on the front of his shirt. "I want you nekkid."

"Do ya now?" he asked, laughter tingeing his words. His hands did a slow crawl up and down her arms.

Goose bumps skittered across her torso, before settling low in her belly. Wetness coated her panties. She wished she hadn't worn any.

God, she loved his touch. "Oh hell, yeah."

His mother approached, breaking the two of them apart with guilty smiles on their faces. "We're headed home, Jacob."

"Okay, Mom. I'm going to stay with Paige for a while."

Nina grinned as she hugged him. "I thought as much."

"See you tomorrow?"

"Yes. We have guests coming in during the early hours of the morning so we'll all need to be onboard for a bit anyway. There are never ending chores on a ranch."

"Love you, Mom."

"I love you too, Jacob. Goodnight, Paige."

"Goodnight, Mrs. Young."

"Nina, honey. Call me Nina."

"All right. Goodnight, Nina."

Nina waved as she disappeared into the darkness. A few moments later, she heard several trucks start and then roll out of the parking lot, leaving her and Jacob standing in the deserted tent alone.

"What shall we do now?" Paige asked, looking around. "Everything is cleaned up."

"I thought you wanted me nekkid?"

"I do, but I think we should take it slow."

"Why?"

"Would you like to dance?" she asked, looking up into his expressive eyes. Lust sparkled in their depths. Lust she could handle.

"There's no music."

She stepped into his arms, placing one on his shoulder and cupping his left hand with her right. They slowly swayed. "Sure there is. Listen to the frogs, the crickets and the owls." She stepped closer so her breasts brushed the front of his shirt. Her nipples pebbled into hard peaks at the friction.

"Paige," he whispered, bending his head.

The slow slide of his lips glided across her skin until he reached the crook of her neck. "Jacob." The nibble of his teeth on her flesh drove her desire to explosive. Stickiness coated her thighs. She wanted him. No doubt about that.

"Where do you want to go?"

"Back to my place?"

"Okay."

"You'll ride with me."

She liked that idea. A smile crossed her lips as a plan began to form in her mind of how she could torture him all the way there and make him want her more than any woman he'd ever been with. "Okay.

Just let me grab my purse." She disappeared around the back of the tent where she'd hidden her purse, stripped off her panties and stuffed them inside the receptacle. *Let's see what he thinks of this.*

Several minutes later, he opened the door to his truck and helped her inside with a hand against her behind.

"You are goin' commando?"

She giggled as she glanced over her shoulder. "I thought it would spice things up a bit."

His cock strained against the front of his pants already. What would be do when she unzipped his jeans and engulfed him with her mouth?

"Thinkin' about you with no panties on all the way home is gonna drive me crazy."

"Oh good. How about when I suck your cock while you're driving?"

"Holy shit, woman. How do you expect me to drive with you doin' somethin' so scandalous?"

His eyes glittered in the moonlight with desire. She knew the look. It said he wanted her. Good, she knew how to please him.

"Oh, I'm sure you'll manage, cowboy."

He gave her a long, slow, melt your panties kiss as his hand slid up under her dress. Two fingers pushed into her pussy as she groaned her need.

"You're wet, darlin'."

Her thighs spread of their own accord. "Hell yeah, I'm wet. You make me that way." He kept pumping his fingers slowly in and out. "You're tryin' to make me come."

"Are you going to or do you need a little more friction?" His thumb glanced off her clit.

"Damn, Jacob. I was supposed to be teasing you."

"You do, honey, with every breath you take you tease me unmercifully."

Her pussy quivered around his fingers. He never hurried the pace, just kept up the slow glide of his hand. "I feel you. You're right there." He pulled out his hand as he smoothed down her dress. She noticed his hand shook, bringing a smile to her lips. He wasn't so unaffected after all.

"So not nice."

"Anticipation, darlin'. It'll be better later when you come apart in my arms."

He stepped back, shutting the door to the truck. She watched as he went around the front of the vehicle to the driver's side, sighing in appreciation. *Damn, the man is gorgeous.* She wanted to trace every ridge of his amazing body with her tongue. Maybe he'd let her tonight. She hoped so. God, she needed him, but she wanted a little slow lovin' tonight. Maybe fast after that.

"What's the sassy little grin for?" he asked, as he slid into the cab and pushed the key into the ignition.

Chapter Seven

"Just thinking."

"About?" he asked, as he pulled out into the street and headed for his place.

The forty five minutes it would take to get there would be a very long ride. "You and me."

"What about us?"

"How I want to do this." She unhooked her seatbelt before slowly sliding across the seat toward him.

"You shouldn't be out of your seatbelt." His grip tightened on the steering wheel.

She worked his belt buckle lose, pushing it aside. Waiting for a moment to see if he would stop her, she grinned as she kept going with the button at the top of his jeans and then the zipper.

"Commando, huh? And you were giving me shit about it."

"I was hoping for a little action tonight although I hadn't anticipated it in the front of my truck while I drove."

"But, baby, it's gonna be so much fun suckin' you while you drive."

"You tryin' to kill me, darlin'?"

"Nah, just love on you a little." She freed his cock from his jeans as they pulled to a stop light. "Lift up." He jerked up his hips while she tugged his jeans down around his thighs. "Oh yeah." He hissed between his teeth as she slowly licked him from base to tip. “So soft.” She circled the head with her tongue. “Salty.”

The tires squealed as his foot shoved down the gas pedal.

“Easy up on the gas, cowboy. You’ll get us busted.”

He slowed as she took the head of his cock between her lips.

“Ah, fuck.”

“Mmm.” She hummed as he canted his hips toward her face. “Concentrate.” She glanced up to see the strain on his face. “You can do it, cowboy. I have faith in you.”

“You’ll pay for this when we get back to my place.”

“I’m sure I will.”

A little bit of suction made him moan so she did it again. Lick. Suck. Slide. *God, I love his cock.*

“Eyes open, cowboy.”

“I am!” He groaned. “I’m gonna blow.”

“Good. Explode for me.”

He pulled over on the shoulder of the interstate and slammed the truck into park as cum shot down her throat.

“Oh God, oh God.”

“Praise be the Lord.” She laughed as she took her time licking him clean.

Satisfied with her work, she started backing away when blue lights flashed in their rearview mirror.

“Shit.” Jacob scrambled to pull his jeans up and button them before the cop climbed out of his car.

She burst out laughing as she slid back into her seat so she could buckle her seatbelt. A moment later, a cop tapped on the driver's side window, then motioned for Jacob to roll it down.

"Can I help you?"

"Just checking on you since you're pulled over on the side of the road. Problem?"

"No sir. I thought I might have had a flat, but it'll be fine until I get home."

"You haven't been drinkin', have you, sir?"

"No, sir. You can test me if you like."

As the cop peered inside, she waved to him. "I don't think that'll be necessary since I don't smell alcohol on you. Be careful drivin' and safe travels home."

"Thank you, officer," Paige hollered from her side of the truck.

The cop tipped his hat before he headed back to his patrol car.

"You are definitely gonna pay for that, darlin'."

Jacob pulled back out onto the highway keeping a close eye on her. She gave him a cheeky grin every time he glanced her way.

"Come 'ere."

"Where?"

"To the center. There's a seatbelt. Buckle yourself in."

"What are you going to do?"

"Tease the piss out of you until we get back to my place."

"Oh?"

"Do it now."

"Yes, sir." She loved when he went all commanding on her. "Whatever you say, Jacob." She unbuckled her seatbelt, slid over into the center and refastened the belt around her waist.

"Lift your dress."

She pulled the skirt up and secured it in the waistband by tucking it in, revealing her thighs to his gaze.

"More. I wanna see your pussy."

Inching the remaining material above her hips, she laid everything bare for his gaze.

"You're gorgeous. You shaved?"

"I thought of you while I did it."

"Sexy." His knuckles turned white on the steering wheel where he gripped it hard enough to strangle the thing. "Spread your thighs."

She placed one foot on the floorboard behind his leg and one on the other side of the gearshift. "Like this?"

"Fuck. You are so hot."

Her thighs were sticky from her arousal. She wanted him. Maybe she could convince him to pull off one of the side exits so they could get in a quick fuck to tie her over. Sweat beaded on his forehead when she glanced at him. "Maybe we could stop on the way home."

"Nope."

"But—"

"I want you to make yourself come."

"Here?"

"Yeah. I'm gonna watch you finger yourself to orgasm."

It sounded arousing even to her.

"Lick your fingers. Get them good and wet. Then circle your clit real slow."

She stuck her fingers into her mouth, making the digits almost dripping wet. "Like this?" she asked, sliding her fingers around the hard nub. *God, I'm so horny.*

"Oh yeah." His breathing sped up. "Now, dip your fingers into your pussy. Feel those muscles gripping your fingers? That's how it feels when I finger fuck you."

She growled deep in her throat.

"Circle your clit again." The instructions coming from his mouth had blood rushing in her ears. Her heart throbbed in a rapid pulse. Her breath came out in little pants. "Rub it hard. Faster now."

The nub hardened more. If he kept this up, she would indeed come all over his leather seats.

"This is so fuckin' hot. You have no idea." The panting of their breathing drowned out the hum of his tires on the pavement.

She continued to rub her clit in a slow, tantalizing motion. Eventually, she would come, but she could do this for a while before she did.

"Faster. I wanna see you squirt before we reach Bandera."

"Squirt?"

"You've never squirted before?"

"No."

"It's when you come so hard, cum literally squirts out of you."

"But, I don't want to do that all over the interior of your truck."

"Baby, it washes. It's leather. Now, make yourself come and if you don't squirt, we'll have to start all over."

She sped up the friction on her clit, driving her desire up so high, she thought she might lose control of her bladder. Stars flashed behind her squeezed eyelids. Heat crawled up her thighs before it centered low in her belly. She felt like she would explode from the inside out. "Oh, God!"

"That's it, baby. Come for me."

She moaned as she felt herself lose control. Cum spilled from her pussy to coat her thighs and buttocks as well as his leather seat.

"Fuck yeah. Gorgeous." The friction on her clit grew stronger as he switched her fingers to his. "Come some more."

She lost herself in the sensation of his fingers on her clit. When he pushed two inside her pussy, she shouted his name as she exploded again.

As she slowly came down from her high, she realized he still continued to slowly finger her clit until she felt it getting hard again.

"Think you can come again before we reach the house?" he asked with a grin.

"No." She sat up when she found herself slumped almost horizontal on the seat. "Do you have napkins in here? I have cum all over my thighs."

"Good." He leisurely removed his fingers and licked them as they drove up to the gate of Thunder Ridge. "Leave it. I wanna lick all that sweetness off when we get inside."

"But it's sticky."

"We can always fuck in the shower."

"Such an inventive guy, you are."

The crooked grin on his face made her smile. Tonight would be off the charts on the sex scale, she could tell. He said he hadn't been with anyone since the last time they'd fucked, but could she trust him? What difference does it make whether he was with someone else or not? It didn't, she supposed, but it would be nice to know he'd suffered while she'd been thinking of him the whole time.

They pulled up to his trailer moments later.

Lights shone from the main lodge windows as she glanced out the front windshield of his truck. One of these days, she would have to get a good look at the ranch. Since she'd only ever been there at night, she hadn't seen much.

"Let me get the door," he said, popping out his side of the truck and shutting the door behind him.

With her dress up around her waist, she tugged it back down to make herself at least a little presentable as he went around to her side of the truck. Paige frowned as she heard the giggle of children's laughter.

When Jacob opened her door, she asked, "Are there children staying on the ranch?"

"Not that I know of," he replied as she slid out and he shut the door behind her.

"Didn't you hear the children laughing?" Although, she didn't hear it now. Not a sound. No rustle of wind or anything. The night was completely still, almost eerily so.

"No."

"Huh. I could have sworn I heard children when you opened your door to come around this side."

"It's probably the ghosts."

"Ghosts? You have ghosts on the property?"

"Yeah, a few."

"Wow. How cool is that!" She took his hand as he led the way toward the door of his home. "Who are they?"

"We aren't sure. We have an old cowboy who hangs out in the main lodge, a couple who argues upstairs and a mother and her children who play in the yard sometimes." He shoved the key in the lock. "The main lodge used to be a brothel."

"Cool." The chilly air of his home hit her in the face like a frigid blast. "It's freezing in here, Jacob."

"Let me kick on the heat. I turned it off this morning before we left for the barbeque." With a whoosh, the air in the room started to thaw. "It'll be warm in a minute." He rubbed her arms. "Should have brought a jacket."

"I didn't think it would be this cold. It's warmer outside than it is in here."

"I'll have you hot in a hurry." His mouth descended, taking hers in a surprisingly fierce way.

Her body warmed from her toes up as he took possession of her. It wasn't a soft, lingering kiss, it was a set-your-panties on fire kiss meant to jack up the heat in her body to inferno within seconds. His lips moved from her mouth to her jaw as she tilted her head to the side with a groan. God, the man could kiss. "Jacob."

"Hmm?" His lips vibrated against her flesh. Next stop, her earlobe with his teeth.

After several seconds, he lifted his head to stare down into her eyes. The dark brown pools sparkled with desire. "I want you naked in my arms in five seconds flat."

His cock strained the front of his Wranglers, tenting the material with his size so she could feel every inch against her abdomen.

She reached for the bottom of her sundress and whipped it over her head.

His eyebrow shot up. "Good girl."

When she moved to take off her sandals, he pushed her into the recliner and knelt at her feet. "I love a man at my feet."

Once her left shoe was removed, he kissed the arch of her foot before working his way up her calf with his tongue. Never in a million years would she thought of her leg being an erogenous zone, but he sure had her toes curling in response to the scrape of his whiskered cheeks and the softness of his lips on her calf.

"You're making me shiver."

"Good." He did the same thing to her right foot. "Spread your thighs. I'm gonna lick you clean."

Her body exploded in goose bumps as her stomach flipped over.

He kissed his way up the inside of her thighs as she watched mesmerized. Her lips parted on a sigh. *Damn the man*. He certainly knew what to do to get her horny, not that she wasn't before this, but what he was doing to her was downright sinful.

His palms slid under her buttocks, dragging her forward in the chair until her pussy was even with his mouth.

"Hold on."

She grabbed his shoulders, digging her fingernails into his impressive width as he swiped his tongue along her slit in one long lick. The moan that broke free from her lips sounded almost primal.

He growled his appreciation as he ate at her pussy like a starving man. At this rate, he would have her coming within seconds.

"Come for me, Paige," he said as he shoved two fingers into her empty center.

Heat exploded through her pelvis in a long, rolling wave of warmth as she groaned his name through clenched teeth. He'd made her come so hard and so fast, her brain went numb.

He lapped at her juices, bringing her down from her climax slowly with long licks until she pushed his head away, not able to handle the stimulation any more. His chin glistened as he grinned like a man who'd just won a gold medal as he sat back on his heels. "Better?"

"I really need a shower now."

"Great." He got to his feet, pulled off his shirt and then toed off his boots. "I'd love to fuck you in there."

"Are you sure there is room? Trailers like this usually have small showers."

"There'll be plenty of room." He swept her up in his arms and carried her down the hall.

She giggled as she wrapped her arms around his neck and buried her nose in the crook of his shoulder. "Mmm. You smell good."

With a flick of his fingers, he caught the light switch, illuminating the bathroom to her gaze. She hadn't noticed the shower stall when she'd been here before, but there wasn't any way they'd both fit in there much less have the room to fuck like bunnies. "We aren't going to fit in there, Jacob."

"You'll be ridin' my hips, babe. We'll fit." He flipped on the water and pulled the curtain. A moment later, his cock sprang free from the confines of his jeans as he pushed them to the floor.

Her mouth watered to taste the pre-cum glistened on the tip.

"*Uh-uh*. In the shower."

She frowned until he swatted her butt. "Ouch."

"In the shower, I said."

"Yes, Sir." She climbed in with him right behind her. The stall was so small the tips of her breasts brushed the expanse of his chest. "This isn't gonna work."

She squeaked in surprise as he grabbed her butt and lifted her.

"Sure, it will."

The minute she had her legs wrapped around his waist he positioned his cock at her entrance. Snapping his hips, he buried his full length inside her, earning him a steady groan.

"Oh, hell yeah." He leaned her back against the wall behind her and began to piston his hips. "God, you feel like heaven and hell wrapped in one tempting package."

"I'm your angel, remember?" She nipped him with her teeth to drive him crazy while he pounded into her flesh.

His feet began to slip on the slick bottom of the shower stall. "Hold on." He pulled out of her, letting her legs slid down until she was standing on the bottom with him. "This isn't gonna work. I can't get leverage in here. Let's take this into the bedroom, babe." He shut off the water and grabbed a towel to dry her with.

"I told you it wouldn't work."

He swatted her on the butt with his wet hand. "No back talk outta you."

The minute she was dried off, he herded her quickly into the bedroom with a palm to her butt. The slow massage of his hand there made her belly dip as he settled her on the bed on her knees. She'd heard about anal sex, but she'd never tried it. The thought intrigued her though. Jacob wasn't a small man by any means.

"Ever had a man in your ass?"

"No."

"One of these days, I'm going to take you there."

She closed her eyes and shivered.

"But not now. This minute, I want to feel your pussy grip me like a vice."

"God, you make me so hot."

"I'm gonna take you from behind. Fast and hard."

"Do it." He positioned her so her knees were barely on the bed, her ass was high and he had the perfect view of everything. "*Uh*, now Jacob." His hand came down hard on her right butt cheek. Unlike before, heat spread from where his hand landed all the way to her clit. "Do it again." For six swats, he switched back and forth between the left and right, making her ass hotter than anything she ever felt before. It stung, yeah, but the pain turned to pleasure the second he stopped.

"Lordy, that's the prettiest ass I've ever seen."

His cock bumped at her opening before he slowly pushed inside.

The low growl coming from him had her pussy quivering for more until he was balls deep inside her. "Fuck me hard, Jacob."

"Love to, babe."

He grabbed her hips in both of his hands and did just that. The slam of his pelvis against her ass almost shoved her across the bed, but she braced herself with her hands wide and her back bowed to take everything he wanted to give her.

The rough sex felt fantastic. She needs this, wanted this with him unlike any man she'd ever been with before. They treated her like a princess, but she didn't want to be treated like a fragile flower. She wanted to be treated like an equal.

His right hand snaked around her hip to find her clit. "I know you can come again."

"I don't think so."

"Oh, yes you can."

His finger worked her clit until she held onto the precipice of the abyss by her fingernails. "Ah, God."

"See. Come for me, Paige."

"Fuck yeah."

The sucking sound their bodies made as he brought her to the best climax of her life, made her realize she'd never had sex like this before. With Jacob it was different, he was different. What they had between them could be classified as meaningless sex, but she didn't think so. Their connection went beyond that.

To what?

Chapter Eight

The horse Jacob rode plodded along at a slow clip. It moved beneath him as he shifted his weight with each step, steadily descending the rocking path they always took the guests on.

The scenery was beautiful even to eyes that had seen it way too many times over the years. Junipers clung to the hillside. Wildflowers bloomed in varying shades of blues, yellows and purples including the native bluebonnets of the area. He could see several of their neighbors' places in the distance from up here. The beginning of the tourist season was upon them and he'd been the unlucky bastard to take the group out riding this morning on the ranch. At least the heat wasn't too bad yet. It would be worse later in the day while he was doing some other mundane task on the ranch like shoveling horse shit or stacking hay.

He wanted to kick the horse's sides and feel the wind rustle his hair, like the way Paige ran her fingers through it. Even though the length wasn't too long she did seem to enjoy fingering it.

Paige. Hmmm. What to do about her?

He'd driven her home early this morning after they'd had a couple bouts of explosive sex. With a kiss goodnight and a promise to call, she'd disappeared behind the door of the little house she shared with her father, leaving the scent of wildflowers behind her. He'd stood like an idiot on her steps, until the light had come on upstairs in what he assumed to be her room. The outline of her form reflected against the drapes had the blood rushing to his groin. The ride home hadn't been a pleasant one while he fondly remembered eating her pussy until she'd screamed his name in ecstasy. *God, my name on her lips is a turn-on.*

He frowned, shifting in the saddle to relieve the sudden presser against the fly of his jeans. Yeah, he wanted her, but what about the future? What about where they went from here?

Let's face it, he was terrified of getting involved on a permanent basis.

After the break up with Veronica, he'd sworn off women until his balls ached and his dick threatened to fall off if he didn't get some sex. His hand could only do so much. Sooner or later a man needed a woman. Enter Paige. She'd certainly brought his blue balls down to a tolerable level, to the point he hadn't thought about another woman in months.

His mind wandered to the last time he'd seen Veronica as she dropped the bombshell on his heart.

It had been over a year, his child would have been born by now. His gut ached with the knowledge he would never hold that baby in his arms, carry them around, feed them, change them or anything else. Yes, they'd made the decision together to abort the pregnancy, but really she hadn't given him much choice in the matter.

"It doesn't make sense, Jacob," Veronica said. "I don't want a baby and neither do you."

"But, I do."

"No you don't. You live in a single-wide trailer on your parent's property, work on their ranch and live on what little income you get from doing

whatever it is you do around there. I want more. I want a man who is going places. You know, someone who lives in a big house, has a nice car, and can afford to raise a child. I don't want to live in a trailer. I've done that my entire life."

"In other words, I was good enough to fuck, but not good enough to be the permanent man in your life."

"I like you, Jacob. I really do, but yeah. Besides, I sure don't want a baby right now."

"How can you think of abortion? You'd kill our child?"

"I don't think of it like that. It's my body and I can do what I think is best for me. Marrying you and raising a baby isn't it. I have plans…big plans."

Without his knowing, she'd made an appointment and aborted the child. She'd called him two days after to tell him it was done.

That's when the drinking started. At first it was to drown the sorrow he felt for the loss of his child, but it became a way to deal with the guilt of not stopping her. Of not doing what he could to keep her from going through with it. When he'd see a baby in a carriage, his heart would break. The sounds of a child's cry almost brought him to tears. Someday he would have a child of his own. Someday he would find the woman he could spend the rest of his life with, raise a family, build a house, and see their children grow into adults.

It bothered him to watch Jeff and Terri as she continued to get bigger with her pregnancy. He'd wanted to be able to touch his woman's belly and feel their child kick. Funny thing was, Veronica's face wasn't the one he saw these days when he thought about having a child with someone, it was Paige.

The heat from the sun pounded down on his shoulders as he wiped the sweat from his forehead with the back of his hand. Soon, they would head back to the house and he could get a cold glass of the lemonade they always kept available in the main lodge. The tangy, tart taste would be heaven right now.

"Hey, mister?"

"Yeah," he answered the twelve-year-old kid riding on one of the gentler mares behind him.

"You been a cowboy all your life?"

"Yep. My parents bought this place when I was little."

"Wow."

Silence for about ten seconds.

"Hey, mister."

"Yeah."

"You married?"

"Nope."

"Gotta girlfriend?"

"Sort of."

"Is she purdy?"

"Yep. Real pretty."

"What's she look like?"

"She has long brown hair, big green eyes and she's a…" *Well shit*. He didn't know what she did for a job outside of helping her father at the church. "Her father is a preacher in San Antonio."

"Oh. So she's a good girl."

Jacob almost choked on his spit with that one. Wouldn't Paige think it hilarious to be labeled a good girl? "Yeah, she is."

"Do ya like her?"

"Yeah. A lot."

"You gonna marry her?"

He pushed his fingers through his hair before readjusting his hat on his head. Kind of a weird conversation to be having with this kid, but what the hell he guessed. "I don't know. I haven't known her long enough to tell."

Jacob heard the kid's mom scold him from behind. "Eric, don't bother the wrangler like that. He's busy making sure we get back to the ranch in one piece."

"It's okay, ma'am. I don't mind."

"You have lots of brothers, huh?" The kid started again and Jacob smiled.

"Yep. Eight brothers."

"Wow. I bet it was fun growing up with a big family."

"Sometimes. Other times I didn't like 'em so much. Do you have brothers and sisters?"

"Yeah, a sister. She's back at the cabin with my dad. He doesn't do horses."

"Too bad. Horses are pretty neat."

"I like horses. What's this one's name again?"

"Whiskey."

"I like him. He's a good horse." The kid patted the neck of the animal.

"Did you check out the pool already?"

"Yeah. I was in there this morning and I want to go swimming again when we get back. This cowboy stuff is kinda hard work."

"It sure is."

"What else do you do?"

"Clean stalls, pile hay, break horses, you know. Cowboy stuff."

"Did you always wanna be a cowboy?"

"Sure did." Jacob smiled again. "What do you want to be when you grow up?"

"I dunno. Maybe an astronaut."

"Sounds cool."

"Yeah, but I don't like to fly."

Jacob swallowed a laugh. "Could be a problem then."

"Yeah. Maybe a scuba diver. I like to swim."

"Good idea then."

"But I don't like sharks."

"They can be kind of mean sometimes."

"Hmm. I guess I have some thinkin' to do."

"Sounds like it, but you have time, buddy. You are what, twelve?"

"Thirteen. I'm a teenager."

Oh shit. Poor parents. "Sorry. You have lots of time to figure out what you want to do with your life."

"How old are you?"

"Thirty one."

"Wow. You're kinda old for a cowboy, ain't ya?"

Jacob did laugh at that one. "No. My dad is a cowboy and he's in his sixties."

"Has he always been a cowboy too?"

"Most of his life, yeah."

"I didn't think you could be a cowboy for a long time like that." A hawk flew overhead. "Those guys who ride bulls ain't very old."

"No, they aren't. Bull ridin' is a hard profession to be in for a long time."

"I think those guys are crazy."

"Me too," his mother added for emphasis. "What did you say your name was again?"

"Jacob, ma'am."

Another woman giggled from behind Eric's mother. He'd seen her when she'd mounted up. Nice looking woman with blonde hair, big blue eyes, and nice tits. She was visiting the ranch with a couple of friends and they had all been eyeing the Young brothers since they had driven in.

Monica. That's what she introduced herself as. They'd been there a couple of days already and if he remembered right, his mother mentioned they were there for two weeks. He rolled his eyes behind his sun glasses.

They came down the final path to the back of the corral and he sighed. Thank goodness the ride was over. As he led them into the fenced in area where the horses were kept, Joey met them. He normally took care of the horses, broke the new mares, and tended to the tack. He'd hurt his leg breaking one of the horses the week before so he was tending to the stock on the ground instead of riding out with the visitors.

"Hey, Joe."

"How'd the ride go?"

"Good. Got a talkative kid, but other than that, nothin' big."

"Great. Ma wants to see you in the lodge." He took the reins to Jacob's horse. "I'll get your gear off."

"Thanks." He swept his hat off his head and wiped the sweat from his forehead again. *Damn, it is getting hot*. "Any idea what she wants?"

"Nope."

He noticed Jason eyeing the blonde woman as he helped her down from her horse. Leave it to Jason to swoop in on a woman ripe for the picking. Jacob shrugged. He didn't care. They could do what they wanted, he supposed. Jeff was the stickler for not messing with the guests, although he couldn't say much now since Terri had been a guest before they got together.

After he helped a couple of guests dismount, he headed for the main lodge to see what his mother wanted. He needed something to drink anyway. The heat had begun to rise outside and more work waited in the wings of a working cattle ranch.

The cooler air of the main lodge hit him in the face as he pushed open the door. He exhaled as he waited for the sweat running down his back to dry before he went to find his mother.

He grabbed a glass of lemonade before he yelled, "Ma?"

"In the office."

He moved around the wooden posts strategically placed throughout the building to hold up the massive structure, and then through the doorway to where the office stood near the back of the huge main room. "You wanted to see me?"

She glanced up at him through the small glasses perched on her nose. His mother was still a stunning woman even in her mid-sixties. A few strands of grey streaked her black tresses, but it only made her look more beautiful. "Yes. I needed to ask you about the hay supply. Did you stack it yesterday?"

"No. I was doing it this afternoon. I had to take a group out. We rode back in a minute ago."

"Good. Let me know when you're done what we have and what we'll need for next week's delivery, okay?"

"Sure."

"How did the ride go?"

"Good. I had a pretty talkative kid on the ride."

"Kids are so cute. I definitely want more grandkids."

"Well Jeff and Joel will have taken care of that in the coming weeks."

"Jacob, sit down for a minute."

He frowned. "Okay."

"Why didn't you tell me and your dad about Veronica and the baby?"

He tipped his head back against the wall behind him and sighed. "How'd you find out?"

"I ran into her mother in town not long after she aborted it."

"You've known all this time and you didn't say anything?"

"I kept waiting for you to tell us. I didn't feel it was our place to bring it up. Is that why you started drinkin' so heavy?"

"Part of it, yeah. I still feel really guilty about not stoppin' her."

She reached over and grabbed his hand. "Honey, it was her decision."

"No, it was our decision, but I should have been able to talk her out of it or somethin'. Ma, it was my child and I let her kill it."

"But, baby, you couldn't really stop her if it was her choice to do it. It's her body. If she didn't want to carry the pregnancy, there wasn't much you could do."

"I guess, but I'll never forget and I certainly don't think I'll ever forgive her for goin' through with it. You know she didn't tell me she was havin' it done until two days after she did it?"

"She probably knew you'd try to stop her."

"I would've."

Nina stood, pulled Jacob to his feet and wrapped her arms around him. “It’s okay to grieve, Jacob. I’m glad you’ve slowed down on the alcohol though. You had me worried.”

“I know, Ma. I’ve stopped all together.”

“Good for you. I’m glad to hear it. What made you stop?”

“A woman.”

“Paige?”

“Yeah. She kept me from gettin’ my ass kicked in a bar.”

Nina tilted her head to the side. “She hangs out in bars? A preacher’s daughter?”

“Yeah, but don’t you say anything to her dad.”

“He doesn’t know, I take it.”

“No.”

“What a tangled web we weave.”

“I know. I wish she wouldn’t keep it a secret from him. He’s bound to find out sooner or later. I don’t think it’ll be a pretty blow up either.”

“You really like her, huh?”

“Yeah, I do.”

“I’m glad. You need a good woman in your life.”

He smiled and kissed her on the cheek. “Don’t be plannin’ weddin’ bells just yet.”

She brushed some hay from the front of his shirt. “I’m not.”

“Enjoy Mesa and Terri for a while yet, Ma. I don’t want you to get your hopes up on me and Paige.”

“She’s a nice girl though.”

“Yeah, she is, but we are gettin’ to know each other right now. Takin’ it slow, you know?”

"All right, baby. I'll lavish my attention on Mesa and Terri for now."

"Thank you. I love you, Mom."

"I love you too, Jacob. Now, back to work with you."

He kissed her on the cheek again before he disappeared out the office door. A quick glance at the leather sofa's in front of the huge fireplace in the main room revealed a cowboy sitting on one of the couches. The man tipped his dusty cowboy hat and disappeared. Man, he'd never get used to seeing the ghosts who inhabited Thunder Ridge ranch. The lonesome cowboy was the one they saw most often especially in the main lodge.

The lunch bell clanged signaling it was time to eat.

The noise level rose exponentially as the crowd poured in from outside for the noon meal. The tang of grilled hamburgers and hot dogs made his stomach rumble. He'd missed breakfast this morning taking Paige back to town.

The blonde, brunette and two redheads from the group on the ride this morning came in to get in line for lunch. Monica glanced his way with a smile. How could a woman look good after a sweaty morning ride without smelling like horses? She wasn't bad looking. A little on the plump side, but he wasn't one for skinny women anyway. Her friends were kind of pretty too. The brunette caught his attention, curvy with nice round high breasts, slim waist, and nice ass. Her shape reminded him of Paige. One of the redheads smiled and waved. Her eyes were a very pretty green, kind of like new spring grass. Paige's were emerald green and sparkled like the stone itself.

Wow. He was really messed up if everyone reminded him of Paige in one way or another.

When the guests had all been served, the family rose as a group to get their lunch. The rules according to his mother, to make their guests feel welcome. He smiled. She had a lot of rules. No messing with the guests. No eating before the guests. Treat them with respect, but flirting wasn't out of the question. Make them feel welcome. *Sheesh.* Of course, they had one of the most guest friendly ranches in the area and it showed especially during the summer when they were full all the time.

After they'd all been served and the family sat back down, talk around the table settled into what they had to do this afternoon. He knew he had to stack and count the hay bales for his mom to tally the feed needed for the rest of the week. Stalls needed cleaning too.

Sighing, he longed for a nice cool shower already.

"Are you okay, Jacob?" Jackson asked from his seat across the table.

"Yeah, why?"

"You seemed tired. Late night?" Jackson grinned as he bit into his hamburger.

Jacob knew something was up if his brother had that sparkle of mischievousness in his eyes. "Kind of."

"The pretty green eyed girl from the barbeque yesterday sure had eyes for you this morning when you took her home."

Shit. "Mind your own business Jackson." He should have known. They left early enough, but his brothers were usually up before the sun doing chores.

"I was, but it's hard to miss your laugh and her giggle at six in the mornin'."

"I didn't realize Paige was here last night, Jacob." His mother smiled too as he narrowed his eyes.

She would really push the matchmaking now that she knew things were a little more serious between him and Paige than she'd first thought. *Getting a little sex doesn't mean things are serious.* "Butt out, Ma."

His brothers all glanced his way. He couldn't blame them. He'd never brought a girl back to his place before. Paige had been there twice.

"You brought a girl home?" Jeremiah asked, leaning forward in his chair. "You never bring women back here."

"Let it go. It's nothin'."

"It is something, Jacob," Jeff said. "At least she's not a guest."

"You're one to talk, Jeff. Terri was a guest when you were—"

"Jacob," his father growled in warning. "That's enough."

"And Mesa was a guest too."

"Leave Mesa and Terri out of this," Joel warned as Mesa blushed a deep red. Terri wasn't at the table this morning for some reason.

"Sorry, Mesa. I'm a little touchy this mornin'."

"Apparently."

"That's enough, boys," his father said, taking the tension down a notch. "This conversation isn't appropriate with guests in the room. Let's move onto something else. Joey, how are the new mares working out?"

"Good. Jacob took two of them on the morning run with guests. Jacob?"

"No problems." He shoveled some potato salad into his mouth. At least if he was chewing he wouldn't have to talk. His disposition seemed to be getting sourer by the moment with all the talk of Paige. Things were going good between them. If his brothers started in, she might bolt like a skittish foal. He wondered if her father managed to corral her this morning for a talk. He'd have to call her later.

He frowned. Since when did he really care about how things were going in her personal life? *Since you fucked her brains out last night after a very family oriented day with her.*

"Mom, I'm going to be updating the website this afternoon so the reservations system will be down for a couple of hours," Jonathan said as he shoved his plate aside.

"All right. Thanks for the warning."

Jacob wanted to escape. Even throwing hay would be better than sitting here listening to the mundane conversation around the table with his family. "I'm headin' to the barn."

"Are you all right, Jacob?" his mother asked, glancing up at him as he stood ready to bolt.

"Yeah. I'm fine. I need some breathin' room is all." He jammed his fingers through his hair before he adjusted his hat on his head. "See y'all at dinner."

He tossed his plate into the dirty dish bin as he tuned out the laughter and conversation of the guests around him. The barn would be quiet except for the occasional shuffle of horse hooves, the meow of the barn cat or the rustle of wind through the rafters. Peace. Right now he needed the atmosphere of the barn to think.

The heat of the day would be almost oppressive in there, but he needed to work off some of this nervous energy. His muscles twitched and bunched as he walked with a purposeful stride toward the large structure at the back of the property. The main compound consisted of the large lodge and several guest cabins. Each cabin had two sides connected with a door between them so they could be opened up for a larger group. There were four of these double cabins as well as rooms in the main lodge where guests stayed.

Right now he wanted to be away from everyone.

He stepped into the shadowed doorway of the barn inhaling the scent of hay, manure, and leather, letting it calm his restless soul. Dust danced in the sunlight coming through the rafters above his head, illuminating pieces of hay on the ground at his feet. Horses shifted in their stalls. The scurry of mice along the rafters reached his ears. The barn cats had their work cut out for them. A couple of kittens wrapped themselves around his boots so he leaned down and picked one up to scratch it between the ears. The little grey striped one was his favorite.

"I'm such a sucker for kittens and babies, but you're a cutie, aren't you?" He ran his hands over the little furry body a couple of times before he set it on its feet and headed for the loft.

Leather work gloves sat on the pile of hay to his right. He shoved his hands into the soft kidskin to shield his skin from the rough bailing string around each bale. They went through a lot of hay and feed this time of year.

As he began to stack the bales in the corner, he let his mind wander to what he was going to do about Paige. Everything seemed to be going okay for now, but he wasn't sure where it might be headed in the future. Was there a future for them?

He didn't even know what she did for money to live on. Something he would have to correct. She knew more about him than he knew about her. What was her favorite color? Her favorite flower? Did she like certain perfumes over others? She definitely had a different personality, kind of an enigma so to speak. She rode a Harley, dressed in leather, but didn't drink alcohol. She also had the sweet, innocent, church girl thing down pat from what he saw at the barbeque yesterday. It fit her too.

He grinned as he threw a bale into the corner stack. He sure would enjoy unwrapping all the layers of Paige Tyler.

Chapter Nine

"I don't know what you're thinking anymore, Paige." Her father raked his hands through his greying hair.

When had the grey started to come in? She hadn't really noticed before, but she did now. He seemed to be growing older by the day. It worried her. He probably needed a doctor's visit. He hadn't been to one in years. "Daddy, I just—"

"Honey, what's going on? You're a totally different girl these days. Is it that young man I saw you with so much yesterday? Is he causing this change in you?"

"No. I've been like this for a while."

"Wild?"

She bowed her head. "I'm not wild."

"Yes, you are. You haven't known him long and here you are staying out all hours of the night with him. You came home early this morning. I heard you come in."

"I'm a grown woman, Daddy."

"Really? You sure aren't acting like a mature, young woman doing all these crazy things."

"You have no idea," she whispered under her breath.

"What did you say?"

"Nothing. I'm sorry. I'll try to behave more appropriately for a preacher's daughter."

"You should. This behavior isn't becoming of you. You can't attract a nice Christian man like this."

"Maybe I don't want a nice Christian man."

"Paige." His exasperated voice raised the hackles on her arms.

"I'm sorry, Daddy. I can't be the girl you think I should be. I have to be me."

"And exactly what does that mean?"

"What would you say if I went to bars on the weekends?"

"Instead of going to the nursing home?"

"Yes."

"You lied to me?"

"In a sense, yes."

"Is that how you knew the band members who played yesterday? You met them at a bar?"

"Yes. I don't drink though. I go to listen to the music and dance."

"Dancing too?"

Oh Lord what would he think if he knew I dressed in leather and rode a motorcycle? Confession time I think. "Yes, dancing too. I need to tell you something. I've been going to bars for a few months now. It's how I met Jacob. I saved him from a bar fight."

Sweat popped out on his forehead as he took a seat at the kitchen table with her.

"Are you all right?"

"I'm fine. I have a little nausea at the moment. Breakfast must have upset my stomach this morning."

"You don't look very well, Daddy. I should call the doctor."

"I'm fine." He pressed the heel of his hand to his chest.

"Are you having chest pain?"

"A bit of pressure. Nothing serious." He wiped the sweat from his forehead with a handkerchief he'd pulled from his back pocket. "Back to you. Why do you feel the need to hang out in bars and why did you lie to me?"

"You wouldn't understand."

"Try me."

She clasped her hands together, putting them on the table in front of her as she tried to explain this need to her father. "I need to be around people my own age. Dancing is fun. Hanging out with people is fun."

"Do you really enjoy these things?"

"Yes, I do. I can't always be the preacher's girl. I need to do things people my own age enjoy. I don't want to hang out with the ladies from the auxiliary. The guys in the band are my friends. Jacob is my friend."

"You're sleeping with him, true?"

"I have, yes."

"Premarital sex, Paige?"

"It's common these days, Daddy."

"I never thought my daughter would engage in those sorts of things. What would your mother say if she were here?"

"I'd hope she'd understand as I hope you'll understand." He leaned over and put his head on his folded hands. "I'm calling an ambulance."

"I'm fine," he mumbled right before he slid from the chair onto the floor.

"Daddy!"

He didn't respond.

"Shit." She grabbed the phone from the wall, dialing nine-one-one.

"What's your emergency?"

"My father. He was complaining of nausea, pain in his chest and sweating profusely. Now he's on the floor."

"Is he breathing?"

"Yes."

"I'm sending an ambulance. You'll need to meet them outside."

She rattled off the address, stretching the phone cord far enough she could reach his side and still be on the phone.

"Keep talking to me," the dispatcher said. "If he stops breathing or his heart stops, you'll need to do CPR until they get there."

"No, he's still breathing, but he hasn't regained consciousness." Sirens wailed in the distance. "I hear the ambulance."

"Okay. Hang up with me and go meet them. They'll need to know where to go."

"Thank you."

"You're welcome."

She needed something, someone. She wrung her hands together as she headed for the front door. "This way," she said as the paramedics stepped onto the porch.

"What happened," the dark-haired paramedic asked.

"We were talking and he just collapsed from the seat onto the floor. He's been out for several minutes."

"Any symptoms before that?"

"Sweating, nausea, chest pain, I think. He wouldn't really tell me, but that's what it seemed like."

The paramedics cut his shirt and pasted on plastic sticky things to his chest. His heartbeat blipped over the screen on their machine. They quickly stuck a needle in his arm for fluids. She'd seen enough trauma in the ER to know a few things. It sounded like he had some kind of heart attack. *Great. Tell him about your secret life and send your father into a heart attack. Brilliant.* "Do you know what's wrong?"

"I'm not sure, but we are going to treat him as if it's cardiac related by the symptoms you told us."

"What's going on?" her father asked, his eyes now open. "Paige?"

"You're on your way to the hospital, Daddy."

"But why?" He started to sit up.

"Lie back, sir. We've got you hooked up to some machines to monitor your heart and we're giving you fluids. We'll be transporting you to the hospital in a moment."

"I'm fine."

"No you aren't. You need to go," she said, holding him down by the shoulder.

"All right. I guess it wouldn't hurt to have a doctor look at me."

"How long were you having chest pain before you passed out, sir?"

"I've had discomfort in my chest all morning and a little last night."

Great. After the barbeque I pushed his need to talk out of the way for Jacob. He was probably having a heart attack last night. "You'll be fine, Daddy. I'll be right beside you."

"Thank you, Paige."

The paramedics lifted the gurney they'd put him on and locked it in place. With all the monitors beeping and dinging, they wheeled him out through the living room and out the front door to the ambulance.

"What's going on?" Mrs. Johnson asked, coming from around the side of the church. "I saw the ambulance."

"It'll be fine. We'll let you know when we know something."

"Is he going to be all right?"

"I'm sure he'll be fine, Mrs. Johnson." Paige had already grabbed her keys and her purse off the side table before the ambulance crew had him through the doorway outside. "I'll follow you to the hospital."

Within moments, she was following behind the screaming ambulance toward the hospital, thoughts of losing her dad rushing through her mind. She couldn't lose him too. *I need Jacob.* She grabbed her cell phone, scrolled through the numbers and hit talk.

"Paige?"

"Hi. Listen. I'm on the way to the hospital with my father. I think he might have had a heart attack."

"Which one?"

"University Hospital."

"I'll be right there."

"Are you sure? You don't have other things you need to be doing?"

"Honey, if you didn't need me, you wouldn't have called. I'll be there in forty-five minutes."

"Thanks."

"You're welcome. Be tough. It'll be okay."

"I feel terrible, Jacob. I think I brought it on."

"Why?"

She could hear the jangle of keys and an engine start on his truck. "I told him about my weekends. I lied to him."

"Babe, it'll be okay. He's a tough guy."

"But the stress brought this on. I know it did." Tears began to roll down her cheeks. With her hand on the phone and one on the wheel, she couldn't brush them away.

"Calm down, Paige. You're drivin', right?"

"Yeah."

"Be careful, darlin'. You can't help your father if you're in the bed next to him and if you do that, I'll have to kick your butt."

She laughed through her tears. Leave it to Jacob to make her feel better. This is why she loved him. *What the hell?* She sniffed. "It'll be fine, I hope. Thank you for making me laugh. I needed to talk to you. I really need you to hold me."

"I'll be there soon."

She pulled into the parking lot of the hospital behind the ambulance. "I'm at the hospital. Meet me in the emergency room waiting room when you get here. I'm sure they won't let me back there until they know something anyway."

"Okay. Be strong. It'll be okay."

"Thank you."

"You're welcome. See you soon."

I love you was on the tip of her tongue, but she held it in. This was a new feeling for her and she wasn't sure what to do about it. She really didn't know him well enough to say I love you, did she? The phone clicked in her ear, signaling Jacob had hung up. She bit her lip and slowly laid the phone on the seat next to her purse. *Do I really love him? Wow*. This wasn't something she'd expected to be racing through her heart. *What the hell do I do now?*

* * * *

Jacob raced through the streets on San Antonio, tapping his fingers on the steering wheel of his truck. Paige needed him. It felt good. He liked the thought of her needing him a little too much. What did it mean for their relationship? He wasn't sure, but it was a step in the right direction.

The hospital parking lot came into view. He found the emergency room entrance as he pulled into a parking spot big enough for his truck. His heart thumped in his chest. She needed him. The thought brought a smile to his face even in the wake of this tragedy with her father. He liked being needed, he found. With her being such a strong woman, admitting she needed him had to be tough on her as well.

He jumped out of his truck, locked the doors and headed for the entrance. The double glass doors slid open when he stepped in front of them, revealing the stark whiteness of the room. Even the curtains on the windows were white. Double doors to what he assumed led to the back of the emergency room, sat back against the walls.

Paige stood off to his right, rubbing her arms as she paced in front of the chairs. "Paige?"

"Jacob." She flew into his arms like a bird coming home to roost.

Her tear stained cheeks broke his heart. "How are you holdin' up, babe?"

"Not good." She rubbed her face on his shirt. "You smell good."

"I'm sure I smell like sweat, hay, and horse shit. I was throwin' hay when you called."

"I like it. It's you." She stepped back, but not completely out of his arms. "Thank you for coming."

"You needed me."

"Still. You didn't have to come, but you did. It says a lot about you."

Her green eyes glistened with unshed tears as he wiped the remaining wetness from her cheeks with his thumb. "He'll be okay, darlin'. Was he talkin' when they brought him in?"

"Yes, but he'd lost consciousness at home. I'm scared."

"I know."

"Paige Tyler?" a nurse called from the doorway.

"Yes?"

"Your father wants to see you now."

"Can my, *uh*, friend come back with me?"

"Sure, but you two can't stay long. We're still running tests."

"Thank you."

They followed the purple clad nurse back through the doors, down a long hall to a curtain off area to the left. "In here."

"Do they have any idea what happened?"

"I'll let the doctor talk to you both. He'll be in momentarily." She pushed the curtain aside to reveal her father's pale face lying on the gurney with his eyes closed.

"Daddy?"

He opened his eyes and frowned. “What is he doing here?”

“He came because I called him. Be nice.”

“He’s the one who led you down the road to Hell, Paige. How can you expect me to be nice? You need to find a Christian man to be with, not some hoodlum who hangs out in bars.” He coughed several times, making his heart rate increase enough to set off the dinging bells on the monitor.

“You need to calm down, Daddy.”

“I won’t calm down. Get him out of here.”

“I won’t. I need him here.”

“Then you need to leave too.”

“Daddy!”

“What’s going on in here?” the doctor asked, pushing through the split in the curtain. “You need to slow your heart rate down, Mr. Tyler.”

“It’s Reverend Tyler and I want these two to leave my bedside. Tell my daughter I’m fine so she can leave.”

“I can’t say that, Reverend. I don’t know what’s wrong with you yet. Are you sure you don’t want her here?”

“I’ll go wait outside, Paige. It’s obvious he doesn’t want me here.” He rubbed her arm before he turned to go. “I’ll be in the waiting room.”

“I’m sorry.”

“No need.” He leaned down to kiss her quickly on the forehead, not wanting to disturb her father any more than necessary.

The man started coughing heavily again as Jacob disappeared around the curtains and back down the hall. *Well, that went fabulously. What the hell? Does he really think I’m the reason Paige went to bars? What did she tell him was going on between us?*

He pushed through the doors to find the cafeteria. Coffee sounded mighty good right about now.

"You look lost, cowboy," the receptionist said from behind her little desk. "Can I help you find something?"

"The cafeteria? I could use a cup of coffee."

"Down the hall to your left. It's at the end. You can't miss it."

"Thank you."

"No problem."

The woman seemed nice even as she eyed him with a blatantly appreciative stare, but he couldn't really revel in the look when Paige's father might be fighting for his life right at this moment. Not that he'd looked at many women since she'd come into his life. He found he compared everyone to her these days.

The click of his booted heels down the long corridor sounded ominous even to him. He really didn't like hospitals all that much. They reminded him of sterile, stark environments meant to keep people from interacting with each other. He liked to touch, to hold, or to kiss. Maybe that made him kind of touchy feely, which didn't seem natural for a guy, but it was for him. He liked the feeling of skin beneath his fingertips.

He poured a cup of coffee and dumped in some sugar and cream before heading for the checkout. Once he paid for his cup, he went straight back toward the waiting room. He was there for Paige and he'd be there until she didn't need him anymore.

His cell jingled in his pocket. “Hello?”

“Hey, son. Where’d you run off to?”

“Sorry, Ma. I didn’t get a chance to tell you. Paige called. Her dad is at the hospital in San Antonio. We don’t know what’s going on yet.”

“I’m sorry to hear he’s feeling poorly.”

“I planned to call you in a little bit when I knew more so I could tell you how long I’d be gone, but he kind of chased me out of his room.”

“Oh?”

“Yeah. I’m not sure what’s going on yet, but I didn’t want to upset him further.”

“That doesn’t sound very good.”

“It’s not. I’m in the waiting room for when Paige comes back out. I’m here for her anyway, not so much for him.”

“If you get a chance, tell him we’re thinking of him and praying everything is okay. He seemed like a nice man when we met at the barbeque.”

“I’ll tell him. I’m sure prayers wouldn’t hurt right now.”

“Will do. We’ll see you when you get home or give us a call later to update us when you know something.”

“Sure. Thanks.”

“Be careful, Jacob. There’s a storm moving in from the west. Sounds like we might get hit pretty hard with rain and wind later.”

“I will. Bye, Mom.”

“Bye, sweetie.”

The long line of empty chairs along the back walls looked like a good place to rest his butt so he slid into a seat with a weary sigh. This wasn’t the way he wanted to get out of back breaking, grueling work this afternoon, but he'd take any break he could.

As he sipped the hot liquid in his cup, his thoughts rushed backed to what Reverend Tyler said about him. He definitely needed to talk to Paige and find out exactly what she'd told her father. How could that man think he was the reason behind Paige's apparent spiraling into the depths of Hell? Or something along those lines.

Paige came through the double doors, spotted him sitting in the chairs and headed in his direction. "I'm really sorry about that."

"It's okay. We'll talk about it later. What did the doctor say?"

"They aren't sure if it's his heart or something else. He hasn't had any changes in his EKG so they don't think it's a heart attack, but they are doing chest x-rays, blood tests, CAT scans and other stuff to try to figure it out."

"Well at least he didn't have a heart attack."

"True." She sighed as she sat back in the chair. "I hate this not knowing."

"About what he said in there."

She looked down at her hands before looking back up at him. "Don't listen to him."

"Why does he think I'm to blame?"

Her gaze beseeched him to believe her and understand, but he wasn't sure he could. How could he deal with her not telling her father the entire truth? This could be detrimental to their relationship. What if she couldn't deal with telling her father?

"For some reason he has it in his head, I didn't start going to the bars until you and I met. Not that we met at the bar because I was already there."

"You haven't told him about checking out places like The Dusty Boot, riding your motorcycle or dressing in leather, have you?"

"No. He knows I don't go to the nursing home. I told him I'd been going out to spend time with people my own age. You know, dancing and stuff."

"You didn't correct him about our meeting, did you?"

She grasped his free hand, holding it between her own cold ones. "No. Not yet, but I promise I will, Jacob. I'm not hiding how we met necessarily. I just didn't want to upset him anymore."

"When, Paige?"

"Soon."

He sipped his coffee until he got to the bottom of the cup. Extra sweetness hit his tongue with the last dregs. He grimaced at the taste as he set the cup on the table to his left. "I don't like this. Not at all."

"I know. I really didn't mean to keep it from him. When he started having pain at the house, I panicked. I let you take the blame and I'm sorry."

"But you haven't corrected his misunderstanding."

"I will. As soon as they tell us what's wrong and I know he won't have a heart attack because he finally knows his precious little preacher's girl isn't the sweet, innocent twelve year old he remembers. I know we had the discussion about the fact that we've already had sex, but I don't want to make things worse."

"I know he wasn't thrilled when he found out either."

"He knows I didn't come home until this morning. He figured out we spent the night together again. He's not happy about it either."

"Well there is at least that much. Of course, I'm sure he blames me for that too." He jumped to his feet. "I don't like this, Paige. I don't want your father to think I'm Satan's son come to defile his precious daughter. We're in this together. This is a relationship. How are things supposed to work if he thinks I'm corrupting you?"

"Do you think of it as a relationship, Jacob? I thought we were just having a good time."

"I'm in this for more than that. What about you?"

She climbed to her feet and faced the window as she rubbed her arms.

"Paige?"

"I don't know what you want me to say."

He put his hands on her shoulders as she leaned back against his chest. With his lips to her ear, he whispered, "I want you to say this means more to you than casual sex." The reflection of her face in the glass revealed her slowly closing her eyes, almost like she didn't want to face the reality of their relationship. "I guess you really don't need me after all."

"I do."

"No, I don't think you do or you don't want to face the fact of our relationship moving onto something more permanent. You care more than you want to. I know I do." He dropped his hands to his sides so he could step back. The realization hit him like a sledge hammer to the chest. "I'm going to go now."

"Please stay."

"I think you need some time to think. I'm not doin' anything here, but waitin'. Your daddy needs you and he doesn't need my presence causing more harm than good."

"I need you, Jacob."

"For what exactly?"

"Support?" A tear slipped down her cheek as her breath caught in her throat. "Don't leave, please."

"All right. I'll stay for a while." He wrapped his arms around her, pulling her into his embrace. He loved touching her, holding her, but she really needed to give him some idea if his growing feelings were returned. Right now, he felt like someone had stomped on his heart before they shoved it back in his chest. He didn't like the feeling at all.

Chapter Ten

Paige realized with the look on Jacob's face she was royally screwing this up. "I'm sorry. I'll tell him right now." She pulled out of his arms to head for the door.

"Wait, Paige. It's probably not a good time. Not until they find out what's wrong with him."

"But he needs to know you aren't the devil incarnate come to drag me off to the depths of Hell."

"We'll tell him eventually."

The same nurse stuck her head out of the door. "Ms. Tyler?"

"Yes?"

"The doctor wants to talk to you and your father together."

"I'll be right there." She turned to face Jacob. "Come with me. We'll talk to him together."

"Honey, that's not a good idea. Getting him worked up and upset could make things worse than they already are."

"Are you sure?"

"Yeah. Just come back out after you talk to the doctor. Then we'll face him together once they get him comfortable in a room or whatever they're gonna do."

"I love you."

Jacob's eyes darkened to an almost black as a startled look crossed his face. "What did you say?"

"I love you. I wanted you to know that before I talked to my father because you mean everything to me. Whatever happens won't have anything to do with us. We are who we are and when we're together, it's right. That's all we need to know." She kissed him quickly on the lips. "I'll be right back."

She disappeared behind the doors only to lean back against them once they closed to catch her breath. She certainly hadn't expected to blurt out I love you in the middle of a hospital as they waited for news on her father's health. *Brilliant.* "Oh well." She pushed off the wooden panels to walk down the aisle to her father's bedside. The doctor met her outside the curtained area.

"Let's go in, shall we?"

"Of course."

The color had returned to her father's cheeks as he rested against the pillows. He opened his eyes as she took his hand in hers. A cough raked his body for a moment until he caught his breath again. "What's the verdict?"

"You have pneumonia. You probably passed out earlier at home because of the lack of oxygen in your blood. Your saturations were low when you came in. Now that you've had some oxygen, your color is much better as are your saturations."

"Does he get to go home?"

"No. We'll need to keep him a few days for observation and medication. He needs some strong antibiotics to combat the problem. He would be much better staying here so we can watch him. Monitoring is the best thing for him right now."

"Wonderful, doctor. Thank you."

"So it wasn't my heart?"

"No, sir. Your heart seems pretty healthy. Overall, you seem to be in pretty good health besides the pneumonia."

"Thank God."

"He's watching out for me. Always has, Paige."

"I know, Daddy." He kissed his cheek as she pushed his thinning hair back from his forehead. He looked so much older to her than his sixty years as he laid there against the white bedding.

"We'll get him moved to a room within the next hour."

"Thank you, doctor."

"You're welcome. Rest, Reverend Tyler. It's the best thing for you. No excitement. If you have a coughing attack, your oxygen saturations drop."

"You got it, doctor."

The man disappeared behind the curtain as Paige took the chair next to her father's bed. "They'll have you in a room soon, I'm sure. You'll have to rest and not get too excited."

"I won't." He patted her hand as he asked, "Did that young man go home?"

"No. He's in the waiting room."

He frowned as he pursed his lips in the way she knew meant he was about to lecture her on something.

"You aren't supposed to get excited so stop right there."

"You aren't to see him anymore."

"But Dad—"

"I'll hear no more about it. I don't want you associating with him."

"I'm an adult. I can make my own decisions." Her father closed his eyes in dismissal, refusing to engage in the discussion again. “I’ll be back in a bit.”

“Fine,” he said, not even opening his eyes.

Dread crawled down her spine. She needed to talk to Jacob, but how was she supposed to turn her back on the man she loved?

She reluctantly walked back down the aisle and through the double doors. He waited in the same spot he’d left him.

“What’s the decision?”

“He has pneumonia. They’ll be keeping him for a few days for treatment.”

“I’m glad it’s not his heart.”

“Me too. I’ve already sent up a dozen prayers for a good outcome today.” She wrapped her arms around his waist as she leaned into his chest. “They’ll be moving him to a room soon and then I can go home. There won’t be any reason for me to stay any longer.”

He kissed her head as he pulled her in tighter. “I told you he’d be okay.”

“Thank you for being here.”

“Anything for you.”

They stood wrapped in each other’s arms for several moments while she absorbed his strength.

“Would you like something from the cafeteria while we wait for them to get him a room?”

“No, thank you, but you can get something else if you want.”

“I’m fine. The coffee wasn’t bad, but I’ve had better.”

He pushed her back a little to look into her eyes. She wasn’t sure she liked the look on his face. “About what you said before you went back there.”

"Forget it, Jacob. I didn't mean it like it came out."

"Are you sure, because I'm not sure I'm ready to say it back to you and I don't want it to get awkward between us."

Her heart turned into a blob resting in her stomach. He didn't love her in return. She should have known as much. Really, they didn't know each other that well. She didn't know much about him at all. "It's fine. I meant like a friend, you know."

"Friends with benefits?"

"Maybe, but I don't want things to get weird."

"Okay. We'll leave it be for now."

"Good."

The nurse poked her head out of the door. "Ms. Tyler, they are moving your father up to a room now."

"Thank you." She pulled out of his arms, missing the warmth and security she felt having them around her. "I should see him up to his room."

"Do you want me to come back there with you?"

"No!" She swallowed hard. "I mean, it's okay. I'll be back shortly. There's no reason for you to go up there. I don't want him upset any more than he already is."

"Are you okay?"

"Yes."

"Why do I get the feeling there is more to this than you're letting on, Paige."

"It's nothing, really. He was so upset before he had a coughing fit which drops his saturations. They don't want him excited."

He shoved his hands into the front pockets of his jeans as he rocked back on his heels. "All right.

I'll wait here. After you get him settled, we should go have some dinner. It's getting late."

"You don't have to stay, Jacob. I can get home. I have my car here since I followed the ambulance to the hospital."

"I want to hold you tonight. Is that all right with you? I mean, I don't want to put you out or anything."

She hugged him again, kissing his cheek. "I'm sorry. I'm making a big mess of this whole thing. I would love for you to stay if you want to. I just don't think it's a good idea for my father to see you with how upset he got earlier."

"Can I stay at your place?"

She bit her lip. "I guess so."

He stepped back. "Don't bother. It sounds like you don't really want me around so I'll go. Get your father settled and go home. You probably could use the night alone."

"But, Jacob…"

"It's fine, Paige." He kissed her on the lips. "Take a bubble bath or something. You've earned it with this stress." He turned on his heel and disappeared through the sliding glass doors.

As she watched him walk away, she felt as if her whole world had just walked out the door.

* * * *

Jacob slammed his hand down on the steering wheel of his truck as he drove out of San Antonio headed for home. "Why didn't I say it back? I mean, I care about her a lot, but in love with her?" He shrugged. "Yeah, I guess so." *I've never been in love before. Is this how it feels?*

The long drive back would give him time to think. Something wasn't jiving with her keeping him from seeing her father. *Yeah, he'd been upset because he thought I was the one dragging Paige to bars, but she'd told him the truth, right?*

"What if she didn't tell him? What if she's still keeping our real relationship a secret?"

His head began to hurt with all the strangulated thoughts tangling up in his brain. He didn't want to question her motives, but she sure gave him reason to when she acted so strangely. What a difference a few hours makes. Thinking about last night, reminded him of the feel of her lips under his. Her nipples were hard little knots of flesh beneath his tongue when he flicked them. Her taste was addicting. She felt like heaven wrapped around his dick. Her pussy milked him dry when she'd come apart in his arms with a cry of his name, which he loved to hear on her lips.

His cock pressed against the fly of his jeans, making it uncomfortable to sit.

Before he realized, he'd pulled up to the gates of Thunder Ridge. Home.

Maybe he'd talk to his mom about Paige. She might be able to give him some insight to women. Yeah, couldn't hurt to try.

The main lodge house came into view with its three big dormer windows in the front, long porch with the rocking chairs waiting for guests to enjoy the sunset or sunrise from the wide expanse and the donkeys hanging around waiting for handouts or petting. He smiled. This place really was home to him.

He parked around back by his trailer and stepped out. His mom would be in her office for another few minutes tonight even though dinner had already been served to the guests. The smell of dinner still lingered in the air. He'd have to raid the kitchen later.

"Ma?"

"In the back, Jacob."

He found her right where he thought he would. "Can I talk to you?"

"Sure, baby. What's up?" she asked, turning to face him.

He grabbed a chair and spun it around to sit down. "It's about Paige."

"Go on."

"Her father has pneumonia, by the way. Sorry I didn't call from the hospital, but we kinda had a little spat so I came home."

"I'm sorry to hear that. I hope he's feeling better soon."

"I'm sure he will. They're keeping him a couple of days at the hospital for treatment."

"Good. That's the best place for him." She patted his hand. "What did you two fight over?"

"Well, apparently her father thinks I'm the reason she's been going to bars, which isn't true. We met at The Dusty Boot, but she'd been comin' there off and on for several weeks. I vaguely remember seein' her there before she saved my ass."

"She didn't correct his misguided notion?"

"No."

"Hmm."

"I thought maybe you could give me some insight to how women think."

She laughed as she leaned back in her office chair. He didn't think the subject was that funny, but apparently she did as she rolled with laughter. "I truly wish I could help you, honey, but I don't know what to tell you."

"I wish I knew what was going through her mind." He sighed as he thought about how much he wanted a drink right now. "She told me she loved me at the hospital."

"How fantastic! Another daughter-in-law."

"Don't rush things, Ma. I didn't say it back."

"Do you love her?"

"I'm not sure. That's why I wanted to talk to you."

"What do you think?"

"I think about her all the time." He leaned forward in the chair, dangling his hands between his legs. "I want her with me every waking moment of every day. I haven't really looked at another woman without thinking about Paige and wondering how she compares. She doesn't. She beats any woman I looked at, hands down. Being with her makes me happy beyond my wildest dreams."

"Sounds like love to me."

"Really? Because I'm not so sure."

"Why don't you think you're in love with her?"

"Because I've never been in love before. I don't know if this is how it feels or not."

She put her hand on his cheek. "Honey, if you can't imagine the rest of your life without her in it, it's love."

"Then I guess I'm in love with her."

"I bet she'd love to hear you say it in person."

"Should I drive back to town to tell her? She probably needs tonight to herself. It's been a hard day with her dad."

"I'm sure a night alone would probably do her good, besides, she's not going anywhere."

"Thanks, Mom. I love you."

"I love you too, Jacob. I'll be happy to have another daughter to love on." She brought him to his feet and hugged him. "Grandkids. I want more grandkids. You aren't gettin' any younger, mister."

"I know, Mom. Trust me. I know." He kissed her cheek. "I'll be sure to bring her home for the whole family to get to know better soon."

"You do that."

He walked out into the main lodge room as he pulled his cell phone from his pocket. Should be call her? No, he didn't want to say I love you on the phone. He wanted to do it all special like with flowers, maybe a bubble bath for two. He snapped his fingers. He'd rent a luxury hotel room in town, wine and dine her before he told her he loved her. Women loved that kind of thing.

Would Paige like livin' on the ranch?

Was he really thinking along permanent relationship lines with her? *Yeah, I guess I am.* He could see his life with her, raising babies in their own little house way back off the beaten path of the rest of the ranch. His own little piece of Heaven. She'd sit on the porch, her belly round with their child and rock the other small one in her arms until they fell asleep. They'd have lots of babies. Maybe enough for a baseball team like his parents. Nine of them.

He grinned. Of course, he'd have to convince her of that, but he was sure he could.

* * * *

Paige tucked the sheets around her father as he got comfortable in the regular room.

"This is much better than the gurney they had me on."

"I'm sure it is."

"Not as good as my bed at home though."

"Stop complaining. You'll be fine here for a couple of days."

"Are you sure you'll be all right at home without me there?"

"I'm going on thirty years old soon. I think I can handle a couple of days alone. Besides, I have to work the next two days."

"I'm sure the kids will be glad you're back to work from your few days off."

"I hope so. I love them a whole lot."

"You'll have to give me grandchildren soon, Paige. I'm not getting any younger."

"Oh pish posh. You're still a young man and there is plenty of time for grandchildren."

"I want a lot you know. You're my only child so you must give me several."

She sat on the chair next to the bed. "I'm sure my husband will have something to say about how many there are."

The frown crossing his face worried her. She'd hope to avoid any more confrontational discussions about Jacob.

"Did you tell that young man you couldn't see him again?"

"Well, I…"

"You didn't, do you?"

"No."

"I forbade you from seeing him anymore, Paige. You are my daughter and you'll do as I say."

"I'm sorry, Daddy, but I'm old enough to make my own decisions regarding who I will and won't see. I like Jacob."

"He's bad for you."

"No, he's not."

"I've spoken so I'll hear no more about it." He leaned back in the bed and closed his eyes, signaling to her the discussion was over as far as he was concerned.

She sighed as she grabbed her purse and her keys. "Goodnight, Daddy. I'll see you tomorrow sometime. Rest." She leaned over to kiss his forehead, noting the coolness of his skin beneath her lips.

"Goodnight, Paige."

As she walked out, letting the door close softly behind her, she wondered what the hell she was going to do about her father and Jacob. She loved them both, but could she risk hurting her father over Jacob? Maybe she could keep them apart until her father came around? It was worth a try. She certainly didn't want to tell Jacob she couldn't see him anymore, but she couldn't defy her father either.

Her stomach grumbled and she realized she hadn't eaten since this morning with everything that had gone on. She figured she'd grab a bite on the way home and take Jacob's suggestion. A nice bubble bath would be just the thing she needed to relax. She may even read a book in there while she soaked. She glanced at her phone only to see no missed calls. She'd hoped Jacob would have called her by now to make up after their fight. *I could always call him.*

She scrolled through the numbers on the phone until she found his name. Her thumb hovered over the talk button for several minutes before she shut the phone off and stuck it back in her purse. Maybe it was a good thing not to talk to him tonight. They probably needed some time apart after her bumbling attempt to tell him she loved him. *Really stupid thing to do. He's probably not ready for love with me. I mean, we really haven't known each other very long.*

"Keep telling your heart that, Paige," she said out loud as she walked to her car. "Love doesn't care whether you're ready or not."

Several moments later, she pulled into the local burger house for some dinner. "Cheeseburger, fries and a strawberry milkshake, please."

"Seven-eighty-two at the window, please."

Once she had her food, she sucked some of the milkshake through the straw, sighing as the cold liquid went down her throat until a racy thought crossed her mind. What would it be like to eat ice cream off of Jacob's chest? Hmm. Sounds like an interesting concept. Too bad he's at home.

She glanced at her purse thinking about calling him again, but decided against it. Tonight was for her and her alone. She didn't have to worry about her father, she didn't have to worry about Jacob, and she didn't have anywhere to be except at home in a warm bath with a glass of wine. Oh, that sounded heavenly to her as she remembered a bottle of Pinot she had hidden in the cupboard above the sink.

The church and her little house came into view. She hadn't left the light on when they'd took off for the hospital, so the front of the house was dark and spooky with only the large floodlight behind the church to guide her steps.

She pulled out her keys, juggling them in her hand to find the front door key without dropping her food on the ground when someone came rushing around the corner of the house, barreling into her.

Chapter Eleven

Paige spun around, holding onto her sack of food like a shield as the big ball of fur almost tripped her. "What the hell?"

Ruff. Ruff.

A large yellow dog plopped his butt on the ground as he stared at her with his big brown eyes. His tongue lolled out of his mouth and she could have sworn he grinned. He looked kind of skinny though and wasn't wearing a collar.

"It's mine, dog. Back off."

He barked again before he lay down on his belly with his paws sticking out in front of him.

"Well, crap."

The dog whined and Paige knew she was a goner.

"Where is your home, buddy?"

He rolled over onto his back wanting her to pet his stomach.

She unlocked the door as the dog jumped back up onto his feet, wagging its tail hard enough his whole butt moved. "Well come on in. I'm sure I can find something for you to eat." The dog obediently followed her into the house, staying right on her heels the entire way into the kitchen. "You can't have my hamburger, but I think there is left over spaghetti in here you can have."

Ruff.

"Yeah, I know. You're too cute to be mad at, but you can't stay here, buddy."

Ruff.

She grabbed the spaghetti out of the refrigerator and set it on the floor. The dog didn't move. "Don't you want it? I thought you were hungry?"

The dog sat on his haunches.

She tapped her hand on her leg. "Come here. You can have it."

The dog launched itself toward the plate, eating so fast she thought he would choke on the food. "Oh, you have manners, do you? Wouldn't eat until I told you it was okay."

When it was finished, he licked his mouth, walked to the rug by the sink and laid down.

"Oh no you don't. I'm going to eat my dinner and you need to go back outside so you can find your way home." She pulled her food out of the bag and then spread it out on the kitchen table. When she looked back at the dog, he'd closed his eyes, resting peacefully as if he belonged there. She sighed as she drank some of her milkshake. "What am I going to do with you?"

With a shake of her head, she ate her dinner, glancing every few minutes at her new friend while he slumbered peacefully on the rug.

As she finished chewing her food, she wadded up the wrapper and tossed it in the trashcan sitting at the end of the counter.

The dog never moved.

She rolled her eyes as she got up and headed toward the stairs to take her bath. When she looked behind her, the dog was right on her heels. "So you're going with me, *huh*?"

Ruff.

The dog lumbered up the stairs, slowly following until they both reached the landing at the top.

She shrugged and headed for the bathroom to run the water before she went into her room to get her nightgown.

The dog lay down on the rug next to the tub, staring at her with expectant eyes.

After she grabbed her night clothes, she returned to the bathroom, stripped down and slid beneath the water with an audible sigh.

"Damn. I forgot the wine." She struggled to her feet, wrapped a towel around her wet body and started for the stairs.

The rattling of the front door knob brought her up short. Was something there? She thought she heard hushed voices. She glanced down only to see the dog at her side, hair standing up on end as his ears perched forward. Had he heard something too?

"Shut up you idiot or she'll hear us."

Laughter radiated through the front hallway as the door knob rattled again.

"This isn't such a good idea, you guys. We could really get into trouble."

"It's fine. He'll love it when he finds her in his bed."

The dog growled as Paige backed toward her bedroom for at least a robe. Maybe she could put clothes on before the apparently drunk hoodlums ended up on the floor in her front hall. She didn't care if she kicked their asses buck naked, but they might.

The door creaked open as the bumbling idiots laughed again.

Of course, she might be able to reach her father's room where he kept the shotgun too.

Footsteps echoed on the hardwood floor of the entry way as the men slowly walked inside.

"Damn it. Where the hell is she?"

"Upstairs maybe. I saw a light on in the window around the side of the house."

The dog growled.

"Fuck. She has a dog?"

"We need to leave now, Jason, before we get into trouble."

"Quit whinnin', Joey."

"I have to drive your drunk asses home so I can whine as much as I want to."

Joey? Jason? Why do those names sound familiar?

"This was your idea, Joshua. What if Jacob is pissed off at us for doin' this? He ain't gonna like it, I'm tellin' you."

Jacob's brothers?

"He was in the barn bitchin' like an old woman about bein' alone tonight. He wants Paige. I heard him say so. He's our brother so we're gonna help him out."

"By kidnappin' his woman?"

"I'm tellin' you, they'll both think it's funny as hell," Joshua said, giggling like a school girl with a crush.

Paige rolled her eyes as she slipped on a T-shirt and jogging shorts. They apparently hadn't heard about how she'd saved Jacob's ass in a bar fight.

The dog growled again in warning even though he'd followed her into her room.

Of course, it wouldn't be much work kickin' their asses if they were as drunk as they sounded. Just for fun, she grabbed the shotgun.

She stopped at the top of the stairs and cocked the gun. "Who's there?"

"Uh. Fuck. She's got a gun, you guys."

"Paige?"

"Yeah, who's there I said. Speak up before I blow a hole the size of Texas through your gut and don't think I don't know how to use this thing."

"It's Joshua, Jason, and Joey, Jacob's brothers."

"What the hell are you doing in my house at this time of night?"

All of them laughed as she stepped down a couple of stairs to see the three of them. "We thought it would be funny to kidnap you and take you back to the ranch tonight. Jacob is missin' you real bad," Joshua said with a hand on his chest over his heart. "He was in the barn cussin' and a raisin' hell because he left you here after you fought earlier."

"Is that so?"

"Yeah."

"You three think you can take me?"

"Well sure. You're a girl."

"I'm assuming Jacob didn't tell you how we met?"

Joey squinted like he was trying to bring her into focus. "How's that?"

"I saved him from getting his ass kicked by three guys at The Dusty Boot."

All three men snickered as the covered their mouths. "That right," Jason said.

"Yeah."

"How'd you kick their asses?"

"I have a black belt."

"No shit," Joey whispered. "Can I see it?"

"Some other time. You boys need to get on home, but I think all of you are too drunk to drive."

"Yeah, probably so," Jason said as he swayed on his feet. "But we'll be fine."

She walked down the rest of the stairs to stand in front of the three big men who stood in her front hallway clinging onto each other. "No you won't. I'll drive your asses home so you don't kill someone on the way."

Joey pushed Jason's shoulder. "See! We didn't even have to kidnap her. She's gonna take us home 'cause we's too drunk to drive."

"And I'm going to tell your mother what you planned."

"Aw, shit. Don't do that. She'll kick our asses."

"As she should. Kidnapping innocent women from their home in the middle of the night."

Joey looked at his watch. "It ain't the middle of the night. It's only ten."

The dog stopped next to her eyeing the strangers as if to ask her whether he could chew them up and spit them out or not. "Easy, boy."

"Is he mean?"

"I don't know. He followed me home tonight. He's not my dog."

"He's awful protective."

The dog growled as she put her hand on his head to calm him.

"Let me grab my stuff and I'll take you boys home. Hand over the keys to whatever you're drivin'."

Joshua pulled the keys out of his front pocket and handed them to her. “Yes, ma’am.”

“You boys probably won’t remember anything about tonight.”

“Sure we will. We ain’t that drunk,” Joshua added as she took the keys from his hand. “We were trying to make Jacob’s night better. That’s all.”

“He loves you, ya know,” Joey replied, bringing her to a dead stop.

“What did you say?”

“He loves you. I heard him talkin’ to hisself in the barn.” The words came out slurred from Joey’s mouth, but her heart heard every word.

“Really?”

“Yeah.”

She sighed as she reached for her keys and purse. Her slip-on sandals were conveniently located next to the table. She jammed her feet into the soft leather. “Let’s go.”

The three cowboys stumbled out the door behind her. “You go on home, boy, good dog.” She watched him walk around the house. “Okay, where’s your ride?” Joshua pointed to where he’d parked the truck. A big white pickup with an extended cab sat in the gravel, parked sideways in front of the church. Great. The damned thing appeared jacked up high enough she’d have to step up to get in. *What is it about cowboys and their big ass trucks?*

The three of them started to pile into the cab as she struggled to get into the driver’s seat.

“Sorry.” Joshua came around her side and placed his hand on her butt.

She squeaked as he propelled her into the truck with one push.

"Just helpin' out."

"Jacob ain't gonna like you havin' your hand on her ass, Joshua." A high girlish giggle escaped Jason's lips as he laughed like something caught him funny.

Paige smiled. They were all kind of cute when they were drunk. "Y'all are hilarious."

"I didn't do nothin'. I was helpin' her in to the truck."

"You coulda put your hands on her waist, man. Not on her ass." Joey smacked Joshua in the back of the head when he returned to the passenger side of the vehicle.

"Hey!"

A scuffle ensued and Paige had to roll her eyes. Was it like this every day with nine boys? She could only imagine. "Enough you three. It's a forty-five minute drive back to your ranch. I won't have you rustling around while I'm trying to drive this big ass truck." What would it be like raising that many children? A shiver of fear ran through her at the thought.

The men settled down as she drove them home. In fact, the two in the back started snoring almost the minute they'd left San Antonio. Only Joshua remained awake.

"Do you love him?"

"Who?"

"Jacob, of course."

"I don't think that's any of your business."

"He's my brother. Of course, it's my business."

She let silence envelope them for several minutes before she answered. "I care a lot about him, yes. Love? I think that's between me and him, but right now there are things beyond our control causing issues."

"He's a good guy even though he was drinkin' a lot."

"I know all about his drinking and yes, he's a great guy."

"You could do worse."

"I sure could." She glanced across the cab as he leaned back in the seat with his hat over his eyes. "Do you have a girlfriend?"

"Nope. Don't want one neither."

"Don't you want to get married some day?"

"Maybe, but I ain't in no hurry."

"What happens when you meet the right girl?"

"Then I'll see if it's meant to be."

He sounded pretty sober to her with his talk of meant-to-bes. He really was a nice guy. All of Jacob's brothers were even if they each had their own issues. She hoped someday they would all fall in love with a woman strong enough to corral the rowdy brothers. Those women sure had their work cut out for them.

The ranch gate came into view as she pulled up. "Code?"

He rattled it off as he sat up in the seat. "It's on the box."

"Oh yeah. I didn't see it." She punched in the code and watched as the wrought iron gate swung wide. Darkness settled outside the headlights of the vehicle making the surrounding scenery almost spooky. She remembered the laughing children she'd heard before and wondered if they would make a reappearance tonight. She didn't really believe in ghosts, but she didn't have an explanation for the sounds she'd heard either.

"I love this place."

"Did you all grow up on the ranch?"

"For the most part. Jacob and Jeff were little when my parents bought the place. The rest of us were born and raised here. It's home."

"I kind of think of the house my dad and I live in as home. We've been there a number of years."

"What happened to your mom?"

"She was killed by a drunk driver several years ago."

"I'm sorry."

"Thank you. I wish more people would find a designated driver when they've been drinking."

"Now, I'm really sorry we showed up at your house. Thanks for bringing us home. You were right. None of us should have been drivin'."

"No, you shouldn't have and you're welcome."

They drove up to the low wall surrounding the front of the main lodge house. Beams of light reflected out the three dormer windows in the front, illuminating the front yard with a soft glow. One of the rockers moved slowly as if someone sat in it, pushing it with their foot in a rhythmic rocking motion. *Weird.*

The two cowboys in the backseat sat up with a snoring snort. "Are we home?"

"Yes."

The three men tumbled out, almost falling on their faces in the gravel driveway. "I hope you three are headed to bed to sleep it off."

A tall, broad shouldered silhouette came out of the barn, heading straight for them.

"Paige?"

"Look, Jacob! We brought her home for you." It was Jason's turn to laugh hysterically at their situation.

"Looks like she brought you home, not the other way around." He pushed his hat back on his head. "What the hell is going on here?"

"We was gonna kidnap her for you," Joey replied, swaying slightly on his feet.

"Paige?"

She dropped the keys to Joshua's truck in his hand. "They showed up at my house, drunk off their asses saying they were going to kidnap me and bring me back here for you since you were so upset about our fight earlier that you were cussin' and raisin' hell in the barn."

"You three were out drivin' like this?"

"Yep. Sorry," Joshua answered. "Good thing Paige brought us home."

"Damn right. You coulda killed someone, you idiots."

"Hey! You're one to talk. You were drinkin' pretty heavy up until a few months ago. You drove drunk several times if I remember right."

"Yeah, I did, but I've learned my lesson. I sure don't do it anymore."

"It was a mistake, Jacob. We didn't mean nothin'." Joey sat down on the low rock wall, leaning back into the grass behind him.

"I hope you three don't ever do this again. It was a really stupid move."

"Sorry," the three of them mumbled in unison.

"I planned on letting your mother know about this little incident, but I think they've been chastised enough."

"Thanks for bringing them home. Do you want me to give you a ride back to town?"

She stepped close enough she could smell the hint of leather, hay, and man. *God, I love that smell on him.* "Do you want me to leave?"

"Hell no, woman. Are you crazy?"

"Shall we discuss this further at your place?"

Jacob grabbed her hand and literally dragged her across the yard, around the back of the main lodge and up the stairs of his trailer. "Does this answer your question?" His mouth dove for hers, trapping her lips in a demanding kiss meant to melt her panties.

When they came up for air, she noticed her heart pounding in her ears as excitement thrummed in her veins. In the heat of the kiss, she'd grabbed his T-shirt, holding him close with a fist of material in her hand.

"I ain't goin' nowhere, darlin'," he said, backing her into the front room and slamming the door behind them.

"Good." She licked his neck from the edge of his T-shirt to his ear. "I love the way you smell."

"I've been workin' in the barn all evenin'."

"It's sexy." She worked her hands into the waistband of his jeans. "I love this butt."

"Do ya now?"

"Oh, hell yeah."

"I'm glad because I love yours too." He grabbed her ass with both hands, pulling her up on her tiptoes. "I want this ass."

A shiver rolled down her spine. Did he mean what she thought he meant? He wanted to fuck her there? She'd read up on it a bit after his last mention of the topic and it sounded kind of kinky and hot at the same time. She wanted to give it a shot, but her ass squeezed together with a little fear of the unknown.

He reached for the bottom of her top and pulled it over her head in one fell swoop, exposing her nakedness to his gaze. "I love your boobs. They fit perfectly in my hands. So round. Nice perky nipples pulled into tight little points." He rubbed one with his thumb. "Horny, baby?"

"I'm always horny around you, Jacob." She pushed his hat off his head, letting it fall to the floor.

"Good because I'm hard as a damned boulder for you."

He pushed one hand down the front of her jogging shorts. One finger glanced off her clit, bringing her up on her toes in a rush of sensation. Her pussy flooded as he slid further down to scoop up some of her cream and spread it around her clit.

"You *are* wet."

"Fuck me, Jacob."

"Oh, I plan to." He removed his hand, lifted her into his arms and headed down the hall to his bedroom. "I'm gonna fuck you six ways to Sunday, baby. I hope you don't have anywhere else to be."

She nipped at his neck, earning herself a soft groan from his lips. "Only right here with you."

When he reached his room, he dropped her legs so she could stand in front of him. "Get them shorts off, darlin'."

She'd lost her sandals in the living room somewhere, so it was easy to drop the shorts in one fell swoop.

"God, you're gorgeous." He traced a finger from her jawline, across her shoulder, down her chest until he reached her nipple. "You got a little sun the other day at the barbeque. You're pink."

"My skin is pretty fair."

"You need sunblock."

"I was wearing sunblock." She leaned into his touch. "Kiss me."

"I plan to kiss you, lick you and eat you all over."

She pushed her fingers into his hair so she could drag his head to her straining nipple. "Go for it, cowboy." When his mouth closed over the protruding point, she came up on her toes to push it further into his mouth. "So good." He flicked the opposite one with his fingernail, earning himself a hearty groan from her. The rough calluses on his hands abraded her skin as he slid it down her abdomen to the curls between her thighs. *Touch me.*

He backed her against the bed, releasing her nipple long enough to push her down on the comforter. "Spread your thighs for me."

When she opened her legs, he dove for her pussy with a deep growl. She giggled at the primitive sound escaping his lips. He sounded animalistic in his need for her. Did he feel as overwhelmed by their connection as she did? She hoped so.

His tongue danced over her clit, down to her slit, and back up. He moaned his delight in her taste. "This pussy is all mine."

"Yours." Her body felt like a guitar string strung too tight. If he plucked it just the right way, she'd break with a sharp twang. "Oh God."

He shoved two fingers into her pussy, stroking it in a slow, torturous rhythm, not fast enough to get her off quickly. He obviously planned to string this out until she snapped.

"Please."

"Please what?"

His tongue did wicked flicks that made her toes curl. "Don't tease me."

"I'm not. Hold off the climax, babe. It'll make it that much better."

"I hate you."

He chuckled as he flattened his tongue and drove it hard against her clit. Heat spiraled through her abdomen.

"I'm gonna come."

His wicked tongue stopped as he kissed the inside of her thigh on both sides. "Easy, girl."

Why did she get the feeling he was calming her like he would a skittish mare? Probably because he was.

She sighed as her body slid into a calm, floating state. Her pussy throbbed for the pressure of his mouth, but he wasn't giving into her whimpers. "Jacob, please make me come."

"In a minute." He leisurely licked her clit, shooting her immediately to incredible need in a second, but not enough to come.

"God, please."

Two fingers drove straight in as he sucked her clit between his lips. She exploded in a spattering of lights and sounds loud enough to deafen her before floating on a cloud of sensation. Her whole pussy quivered, sucking at his fingers when he slowed the rhythmic slide. She wanted more. She needed more.

"I want you inside me."

He quickly stripped out of his shirt, slid those tempting jeans off his hips in one fell motion and kicked them quickly across the room. “I’m comin’ home, Paige. Take me inside you.”

With the head of his cock at her entrance, she enveloped his hips with her thighs as he slipped his cock in, pushing deep.

Their bodies were meant for each other. There wasn’t any way she could ever let this man go.

Chapter Twelve

"You know I planned on a nice romantic way to do this, but you're ruinin' all my plans."

"What's that supposed to mean?"

"I love you. I want you in my life, Paige. You mean everything to me."

"Oh God." She pushed him back so he had to slip out of her. *Now what the hell am I gonna do? What will daddy say?*

"That doesn't sound like you're happy to hear me say I love you."

"It's my father."

"What about him? I know he doesn't like me at the moment because he thinks I'm corrupting his precious daughter, but as soon as you tell him the truth, things will be fine."

She bit her lips before she blurted out, "He forbade me from seeing you, Jacob."

"When the hell did this happen?"

"At the hospital."

He jumped to his feet. "When were you gonna tell me this little piece of news?"

"Soon. I was trying to figure out how to handle this."

"The hell with that. I love you." He shoved his hands through his hair. "We're gonna be together. He'll just have to get over it."

She sighed as she pushed herself up to sit on the bed. "He's a sick man." With her arms wrapped around her knees, she chewed the inside of her mouth as she tried to think of a way out of this mess. "I can't just drop this on his lap."

"He'll be fine, Paige. It's pneumonia, not his heart."

"I know, but pneumonia can still kill a person. What if he gets worse?"

Jacob wrapped her in his arms as she put her head on his chest. "Antibiotics will make him better."

"Let's just keep this between us for now, okay? Let him get over this bout of sickness before we drop this bomb on him."

"I don't want to keep things a secret, Paige. I love you."

"I love you too, but I think this is best. We can still be together here and there."

"Here and there? You sound like you don't have time for me."

"Well I still have to work and do things around the church. I'll be with you as much as I can."

"You know. I don't even know what you do for a livin'."

"I teach pre-school kids."

His fingers did a slow crawl from her elbow to her shoulder, forcing goose bumps along the surface as they moved. "What's your favorite color?"

"Blue."

"Favorite flower?"

"Daisies." She glanced up into his eyes. "Why all the questions?"

"I realized the other day I don't know much about you. You know, those little things one should know about the person they're in love with."

"We have the rest of our lives to learn about each other."

"Yeah, but I've known you for goin' on six months. I should know these things."

"Wow, a whole six month, *huh*?" He rolled her over on her back and startled tickling her sides. She squealed as she laughed hard enough to snort like a pig. "Stop it!"

"No." He tickled her more. "I like when you giggle."

"Jacob! I'm going to kick your ass! Stop!" He pushed her hands up over her head and captured her left nipple between his lips. Her laughter turned to moans. "That's not fair."

His mouth left her breasts with a pop. "Why not? I like the way you taste."

"I thought you wanted my ass."

His eyebrow shot up over his right eye. "Are you going to let me?"

"I want to try it, but you'll have to go slow."

"I will, baby. We'll use lots of lube."

He jumped off the bed heading into the bathroom so fast, her head swam for a minute. *Damn, the man has a nice, tight ass.*

Seconds later, he returned with a white tube. "I'll make sure you are so horny, you'll love this."

Trepidation rolled down her back as she glanced at his ever growing cock. He wasn't a small man by any stretch of the imagination. Would it fit without tearing her apart? He pulled out the nipple clamps she hadn't seen since the first night they were together. "What do you plan to do with those?"

"Put them on your pretty nipples." He leaned over her and captured a nipple again, bringing it to an achy point before he clamped the alligator clip on the protruding point.

"Ouch."

"Too tight?"

"No. I think it's okay."

Nipple number two enjoyed the sensation a little too much, she decided as her body started to hum from the pressure on the hard little nubs.

"We'll leave them on a bit longer this time."

He licked the tips, drawing a deep moan from her. Her clit began to fill with blood. "Fuck."

"I wish I had another one to put on your clit."

"Oh, hell no."

"Hell yeah."

An evil smile spread across his lips as his eyes began to sparkle with a devilish glint. She could almost believe he was the devil incarnate with the look on his face right now. Were those horns she saw? She shook her head to dispel the look. No, this was Jacob. The love of her life.

She spread her thighs when he pushed her knees apart so he could settle there. His tongue began a rapid flicking over her clit, bringing her to the brink of a mind blowing orgasm within seconds. Her nipples throbbed. Her clit throbbed. Everything hummed to the blood rushing in her ears as heat spread from her toes and burst through her belly in an all-consuming orgasm meant to take her breath away. "Ah, God!"

He lapped at her pussy like he never meant to stop.

Once she came down from her high, he rolled over onto her stomach and pulled at her hips until she hung half off the side of the bed. A cold dollop of lube hit her ass, making her hiss at the sensation. "Damn, that's cold."

"It'll warm up real fast once I start fuckin' you there." He pushed a finger into her ass.

She hissed at the burn. How would she be able to take him if one finger hurt? "I don't know about this."

"Relax. You'll do fine." He pushed two fingers in, scissoring them to stretch her hole. "If you want to stop, let me know."

His words helped to relax her into the sensation of having his fingers in her butt. Oddly, it didn't hurt anymore as he spread the lube around and finger fucked her ass for several minutes.

"Ready?"

"Not really, but go ahead."

The hard head of his cock bumped against her ass. The burn made her suck in her breath and hold it. "Breathe, baby. Relax."

"I'm trying, Jacob." She lifted up on her hands and knees when his hand snaked under her to flick her right nipple.

"I know."

He unhooked the nipple clamp, causing the blood to rush back into the tortured tip in a rush. "Fuck!"

His cock pushed into her butt farther as her nipple throbbed from the blood coming back, taking her mind off the pain in her ass. She felt the odd sensation to press back against his groin. "More."

He chuckled as he removed the clamp on the other nipple.

"Damn it!"

"Such language."

"Those fucking hurt, but God I need more."

"I'm in. Oh, Lord, you feel like heaven."

"God, Jacob. Fuck me."

He began moving slowly against her ass. The sensation was something she couldn't describe. She felt full, but empty. She needed more. With a little wiggle, she earned a growl from the man behind her.

"Don't move or I'm gonna blow too fast. I can't handle how you feel."

"It's a weird feeling."

"I can't wait, Paige. You have to come with me."

"I don't know if I—oh." He increased his pace to a jagged thrusting, bringing her to an explosive orgasm as he reached around and pinched her clit.

Jacob groaned behind her, shifting his hips in a slower rhythm now that he'd come. "You're amazing."

He slowly pulled out of her and headed to the bathroom. She collapsed face down on the bed with a moan. A moment later, he rolled her over and cleaned her up with a warm, wet washcloth.

"You didn't have to do that." The washcloth felt soft on her abused tissue.

"But I wanted to. I bet you're kind of sore now, so it's my turn to take care of you."

"You're so sweet."

He leaned over and kissed her abdomen. "And you are fantastic. Thank you."

"For what?"

"Letting me do that. I know it's kind of uncomfortable especially the first time."

"It was pretty awesome. I haven't come so hard in my life."

He chuckled. "I'm glad you enjoy it then. We'll have to do it again some time." He returned the washcloth to the bathroom before snuggling her under the sheet and pulling her into a tight embrace.

Night sounds surrounded them. Crickets echoed in the distance. An owl hooted.

Faint in the distance, she heard children giggling.

"It's the kids. Ignore it."

"It's hard. How do you deal with it all the time?" she asked, running her fingertips through the hair on his chest.

"I don't hear it most days, even when others do. I guess I'm used to it." He laughed. "You should be worn out."

A yawn escaped her mouth. "I am."

"Then drift off and let dreams of us surround you."

"Aren't you the poet these days."

"Love does that to a man."

Within moments, she heard the soft snores of the man beside her and smiled. She really did love him. The question remained, how to get her father to love him too.

* * * *

The next morning, Paige woke up in an empty bed. Birds chirped outside as the sun blazed through the curtains on the windows. She stretched the muscles of her back like a cat in the sun while she wondered where Jacob ran off to. It had to be early yet.

The smiling man of her dreams came through the doorway wearing nothing but a worn pair of sweat pants, and he was still sex on a stick.

"I brought coffee."

"You are my knight in shining armor, sir." She reached for the cup, but he held it away from her.

"Not before I get a kiss."

"Oh, well then." She let the sheet drop as she stood on her knees and pressed her lips to his. She took her time tracing his lips with her tongue before nipping at his bottom lip in order to tangle with his tongue.

He quickly leaned over to set the coffee cup down on the nightstand before he cupped her face with his hands and deepened the kiss to overwhelming. With a giggle, she broke away from him. "Coffee."

"Fine." He handed her the cup. "I guessed cream and sugar, since I didn't know how you took it."

"Good guess." She sipped the hot liquid. "It's perfect. Thank you."

"You're welcome." He stepped back and dropped his pants.

"Now?"

He chuckled. "Insatiable are you?"

Tilting her head, she said, "If you insist."

"Actually, no, babe. I have to get some work done. It's already getting late and everyone will wonder where I am. Breakfast is served in the main lodge in about an hour. You can take a shower and meet me in there if you want."

She frowned at the thought of facing his family after spending the night at his place.

"What's wrong?"

"I don't want your family to think I'm a slut, Jacob. Spending the night with you makes me sound loose."

He smacked her butt. “Stop that, right now. You aren’t a slut. We love each other. My family will love having you as a part of it so stop with the self-doubt.”

“I’m just not used to being around a big family.”

“They loved you at the barbeque.”

She pulled her shoulders back and kissed him on the lips. “It’ll be fine. You go on and get what you need to get done finished. I’ll take a shower and meet you in the main lodge when the bell goes off.”

“That’s my girl.”

He slipped on a pair of jeans and shirt before he kissed her quickly and disappeared out the bedroom door. Paige leaned back against the headboard as she sipped the coffee he’d so thoughtfully brought her. She could do this. Facing his family wouldn’t be that difficult, surely. After all, she’d met them all at the barbeque and they seemed like nice people.

But how are they going to feel after you come strolling out of his place wearing the same clothes you did last night?

She glanced at her tattered shorts lying on the floor. Such wonderful attire to be having breakfast with your boyfriend’s family in. Maybe she should make an excuse and get him to take her home. She could always return for lunch or dinner and she really did need to check on her father today. *But first a shower.*

Her coffee now gone, she rose from the bed to head for the bathroom. The shower turned on with a flick of her wrist, spraying warm water throughout the shower stall. She stepped inside as memories of the last time they’d been in the shower, swamped her. He’d fucked her hard in here, but they couldn’t finish when his feet slipped on the slick floor. She shook her head as a laugh bubbled out.

Shampoo and condition sat in the corner of the stall. She picked up the bottle, sniffed the contents and smiled. *So that's why his hair smells so good.* After she rubbed some of the shampoo in her hair, she scrubbed her scalp and then rinsed. Conditioner came next before the body wash. She giggled. She'd smell like Axe today.

Eyes closed, she enjoyed the warm water splashing her skin until she felt two hands squeeze her breasts. Screaming, she quickly thrust her elbow backward, jabbing the intruder and eliciting a grunt.

"Damn, Paige."

She spun around, slinging water everywhere. "Jacob. God, I'm sorry, but you scared the hell out of me. Are you okay?"

"Other than a few broken ribs." His breath came out in a wheeze.

"Shit, really? I'm so sorry."

He laughed. "I'm fine. I was kidding. I forgot how touchy you are and quick with your reflexes. I won't startle you again." He grabbed a towel and held it out. "Are you done?"

"Yeah." As she stepped out, he wrapped her in the soft terry cloth. "What are you doin' back here? I thought you had work to do?"

"I do, but I couldn't resist knowing my gorgeous girlfriend was in my trailer in all her naked glory possibly taking a shower without me."

"You need to go back to work."

"I will. Kiss me first."

She leaned up as he pulled her in tighter with the towel. The kiss turned steamy when his tongue dipped into her mouth, tangling with her own.

When she cut him off with a nip to his tongue, he scolded, “Ouch.”

“You need to go back to work, but first one thing.” She dropped to her knees on the floor, undid the buckle on his pants and shoved them to the ground. “I’m gonna suck you off.”

“We don’t have time for that. Breakfast will be soon.” He moaned as she encircled the head of his cock with her mouth. “Okay, maybe we have time.” Another groaned surfaced when she swallowed him deep. “Oh, hell yeah.” She sucked and swallowed, massaging his balls until she felt his legs shake. “You’re gonna kill me, darlin’.”

She sat back on her haunches for a second as she glanced up through her lashes at him and ran her hand along the length of his cock. “You can handle it, big boy.” She leaned in to suck his balls into her mouth, loving the feel of the rock hard orbs between her lips.

“I’m gonna blow, babe.”

“Let me have it, cowboy.” She swallowed his cock head as he squirted cum down her throat in a primitive growl from deep in his chest. She loved to hear that sound from him. It made him seem human when he lost control with her.

His legs almost gave out as he stepped back against the sink. “God, you’re fabulous.”

“Glad you liked it.” She wiped her face discreetly on the towel, hoping he wouldn’t notice how she spit out cum on the cloth. She didn’t mind the taste so much, but sometimes it gagged her. This was one of those times.

“You okay?”

“Yeah. I just need to wash my mouth out.”

"Sorry, babe. If you would have told me you didn't like it, I wouldn't have come in your mouth." He yanked his pants back up and buckled his belt.

"It's fine, Jacob."

He rubbed her back as she rinsed her mouth in the sink. The breakfast bell clanged in the distance. "Breakfast is ready."

"You know. I'm not really hungry."

He frowned. "Are you sure you're okay?"

"I'm fine. I'm just not hungry," she said, heading back into his room to retrieve her shorts.

"Your shirt is out in the livin' room."

"I know." She walked down the hall to get her bra and shirt. "Can you take me home? I really should go see how my dad is fairing at the hospital."

"Sure, if you want me to."

"Yeah." She slipped on her bra and shirt, only to find him standing behind her with a perpetual frown. "Your face is gonna freeze like that."

"I'm just tryin' to figure you out."

"Good luck with that."

"I'm sure." He stepped in front of her and rubbed both of her arms. "If you don't want to eat with my family, that's fine. Just say so. You don't have to make excuses."

"It's not that. I'm feeling kind of frumpy in these clothes. I didn't come here anticipating staying all night with you. I wanted to drop off your brother's and just get you to take me home."

"If you didn't want to stay last night, you should have said so. I would have taken you home then."

This conversation wasn't going well at all. "I wanted to stay. I just didn't plan on it, but I really need to be getting home so I can check on my father."

"All right. Let me grab my keys so I can run you back into San Antonio."

"Thank you." She slipped on her shoes as a knock sounded at the door.

"Jacob?"

"It's my mom," he whispered. "Yeah, Mom?"

"Are you all right? I saw you come back to your trailer and you haven't come to breakfast."

"I'm fine."

"Okay. Will we see you and Paige inside?"

"Well shit," Paige grumbled.

Jacob pushed open the door to find his mother standing on the stoop. "No, Mom. I'm taking her back to town."

"How about for dinner tonight?"

"Sure, Mrs. Young."

"It's Nina, honey. You're part of the family now." She waved goodbye as she stepped back and disappeared down the small walkway to the main lodge.

"That went well." Jacob laughed, but she didn't think it was the least bit funny. "I didn't want them to know I was here."

"Well, I'm sure my brothers told her all about it this morning already."

"Great."

"It'll be fine, babe."

He ushered her out the door to where his truck sat parked near the back of his trailer. At least she didn't have to walk past the main house in her sweat shorts.

Within minutes, they were traveling down the road to San Antonio. She felt like shit. She didn't want to make him miss breakfast with his family, but she just didn't feel comfortable being the center of attention as Jacob's fuck buddy. That wasn't true. She wasn't a fuck buddy. They were boyfriend and girlfriend, right? He'd said he loved her and she loved him, so why was she feeling like this?

He put his hand on her knee. "Are you okay? You're awfully quiet."

"I'm fine. Thank you for taking me back to town."

"Of course, babe. I love you. I'm there for you no matter what."

"Thank you." She leaned her head on his shoulder as she stared out the front windshield of his truck. She still had to deal with her father today, which she wasn't looking forward to. Telling him about her and Jacob wouldn't be a pleasant experience, she knew, but it had to be done. They were a couple, right?

"I love you, Paige."

"I know, Jacob. I love you too. Everything will work out."

"Your father isn't going to be happy about us, but we'll get through this."

"I'm sure we will."

Silence enveloped them for the rest of the ride to her house. When they pulled up to the front, the big yellow dog bounded out to meet them. He jumped up on Jacob, taking to him like they were old friends. "Where'd he come from?"

"He's adopted me I guess. He scared the crap out of me last night, but he was ready to protect me from your brothers."

"No collar?"

"Nope."

"Will your dad let you have a dog?"

"I guess we'll find out. For now, he'll just have to hang around the house until things are settled with my father at the hospital."

"I'll leave you so I can get back to work." He kissed her sweetly on the lips. "I'll pick you up later this afternoon, if that's okay?"

"What about around four? That'll give me enough time to see how my father is doing before you get back?"

"That's fine. Dinner is usually served around five-thirty."

"Perfect." Her cell phone jingled in her purse. "I better check this." When she pulled it out, she frowned. "It's a hospital number."

"Do you want me to stay?"

"No, it's fine. I'm sure it's just Daddy wanting to know where I am. I'll call him back in a minute."

She kissed him again before she backed up to unlock the door. She watched as he walked back to his truck and slipped inside. Her phone rang again with the same hospital number. *Damn.* Her father could be so persistent. "Hello?"

"Is this Paige Tyler?"

"Yes. Who is this?"

"I'm your father's nurse here at the hospital. We need you to come in. There's been a change in his condition."

Her heart jumped into her throat. "What happened?"

"I can't talk about it on the phone. You need to get here quickly."

"I'll be right there."

Chapter Thirteen

Paige rushed into the hospital and straight for the elevator without stopping. She had to get upstairs to see what the problem was. *They'd said it wasn't his heart. What could it be now?*

The moment the elevators doors opened, she sped down the hall at almost a dead run toward her father's room.

The doctor stood at her father's bedside when she walked in. "What's going on? I got a frantic phone call from the nurse."

Her father opened his eyes and she could see the facial droop on the right side of his face. His mouth pulled down on that side as well.

"He's had a stroke, Paige. I'm sorry."

"What does that mean?"

"Well there are varying degrees of a stroke. So far his seems to have affected his right side as you can tell by the drop of his eye and lip. He does seem to have some weakness in his hand and foot on that side as well. We won't know the damage for a few days. He'll have to go into rehab."

"What?" She sat on the side of the bed. "How could this happen? He was fine yesterday."

"A stroke is caused by a blood clot traveling to the brain."

"Daddy?"

"I'll be okay, Paige." She understood what he said even though his speech was slightly slurred.

"He won't be able to take care of himself more than likely, but it depends on the damage."

"Thank you, doctor. I'll take care of him, just like he's taken care of me."

The doctor disappeared out the door with a soft click.

"I love you, Paige."

"I love you too, Daddy. We'll get through this." She stroked his hand with her fingers.

"This is going to make me dependent on you, daughter. I won't be able to get around and take care of things for you anymore."

"It's fine, Daddy. I'll be there for you no matter what."

"But this stroke could make things very difficult for you to have a life away from me. I want you to get married and have a family of your own. I want you to give me grandchildren."

"I will, but don't be trying to get rid of me so easily."

"I can hire someone to come in and help me around the house. I think you need to find an apartment or something on your own."

"Are you trying to get rid of me now?"

"No." He weakly lifted his right hand to her cheek. "I need to ask you something."

"What?"

"Do you love that young man?"

"Who?"

"Jacob?"

"Yeah, Daddy, I do."

"Then I won't stand in your way. You need to be with who you love like your mother and I were. I don't like how he has taken you into things that are bad for you, but I'll be there no matter what."

"Daddy, it wasn't Jacob. I went into the bars on my own long before I met him." Tears streaked down her cheeks knowing she was about to break her daddy's heart a little more. "There are a lot of things about me you don't know."

"Like?" he asked, wiping the tear from her face.

"I've been visiting bars for several months. It was my way of rebelling against everything you've been forcing me to do. I don't want to be the preacher's wife and do the duties my mother should have been doing. That's not who I am. I'm me, not Momma."

"I know."

"You do?"

"Yes, Paige. I'm sorry I've forced you to take over those duties. I knew you didn't like them, but you kept doing them anyway so I let you."

"I met Jacob at The Dusty Boot in Bandera. He was drunk off his ass and three men were going to beat the shit out of him. I stopped them."

He laughed, which was a sound she wasn't sure she would hear from her father after everything they'd been through in the last few days. "Leave it to my little girl to save some redneck hell-bent on getting his butt kicked." He coughed several times. "I'm not happy he's a drinker with everything we went through with your mother."

She patted his hand and kissed his fingers. "I know, Daddy, but you've been drinking a lot yourself lately."

"I'm quitting as of two days ago. I won't have another drop."

She smiled as she pressed his hand to her cheek. “Good. Neither is Jacob. He hasn’t been drunk for several months now.”

“I’m glad to hear that.”

“He said after I saved him, it embarrassed him so much that he quit drinking. He used to be such a hell raiser at the bar, he almost couldn’t show his face back in there anymore after that.” She scooted closer. “You know his family. They are nice people, Daddy.”

“I remember them. Big family.”

“Yes. There are eight brothers and a couple of wives in there.”

“Does he love you?”

“Yeah. He told me he did. Not that he’s asked me to marry him or anything, but I think this is the real thing.”

“Maybe I’ve misjudged him.”

“I think you did, but it’s my fault. I let you believe he was corrupting me when it wasn’t the truth. I should have told you from the beginning. I’m sorry.”

“Call him.”

“What?”

“Bring him to me so we can talk.”

“But, Daddy. That’s not a good idea. You should be resting. There’ll be time for a confrontation between you and Jacob when you’re feeling better.”

“I want to make sure he’s going to take care of my little girl. Call him and bring him here.”

“All right. If you insist.”

“I do.”

She stood and removed her cell phone from the pocket of her purse. Once she scrolled through the numbers, she found Jacob's and hit talk.

"Paige?"

"Hi."

"What's wrong?"

"Are you home?"

"Almost. I'm in Bandera right now."

"Can you turn around and come back. I need you."

"What's happened?"

She moved to stare out the window of her father's room. "Daddy's had a stroke."

"I'll be there in thirty."

She sighed in relief. She hated asking him for anything, but she really needed to feel his arms around her right now. "I love you, Jacob. Be careful. There's nothing that can be done for now, but I need you with me."

"I love you too, darlin'. Hold tight. I'll be right there."

She closed the phone and returned to her father's bedside. "He's on his way back. He was almost home from dropping me off at the house this morning."

"What was he doing dropping you off at home in the morning?"

Oh shit. "Well you see, his brothers thought it would be funny to kidnap me and take me out to their ranch last night, but they were drunk off their asses—oh excuse me—butts, so I drove them home."

"And?"

Heat crawled up her neck. Telling her father about her sex life wasn't the most pleasant thing to do. “Um, I stayed with Jacob instead of coming home right away.”

“I’m glad you’re in love with him and he loves you, otherwise I would be having a shotgun discussion with a certain young man about how he’s treating my daughter.”

She laughed as she took the seat she’d vacated to make the phone call.

“I don’t think this situation is funny, Paige.”

“The reason I laughed was because I had the shotgun out last night when his brothers broke in.”

“They broke in?” he asked, his eyes wide with alarm as he fiddled with the blanket beneath his hands.

“Not really. The door wasn’t locked yet.”

“This family sounds like a pretty rowdy bunch. Are you sure you want to get involved with them?”

“Do I have much choice? I love him.”

“I guess I have to deal with a rowdy bunch of rednecks being my in-laws?”

“There’s no wedding planning going on yet, Daddy. Besides, you met his mother and father at the barbeque. They weren’t a bunch of rowdy rednecks there.”

“No, but it was a church picnic. I would hope they were on their best behavior in the house of the Lord.”

“I’m sure they were.” She stood back up. “I’m going to get some coffee and some breakfast. I’ll be back in a bit.” She wanted to head Jacob off before her father got ahold of him anyway, so she figured it would be best to hang out down by the front doors.

About thirty minutes later, Jacob came skidding in on his cowboy boots through the front door. "Paige, what's wrong?"

She sat him down on the bench so she could brief him. "Daddy's had a stroke. They called me right after you left me at the house."

"How's he doin'?"

"Okay, but he's got some weakness on the right side. He'll have to go to rehab for a while to regain his strength."

"I'm sorry, darlin'. I wish I could have been there when you got the call."

His arm went around her as she placed her head on his shoulder. "It's okay. We didn't know this would happen. There isn't anything you could have done anyway."

"Except be here for you."

"You're here now. That's what counts."

They sat together for several minutes before he shifted to the side to look into her face. "So why didn't you let me come up to the room?"

"Busted, *huh*?"

"Yeah. I didn't expect you to be down here."

She caught her lip between her teeth for a minute as she sighed. "Daddy knows about us."

"I knew that before. He didn't like me very much."

"No, what I mean is he *knows* about us. I told him the truth about the bar."

"And?"

"He understands, sort of. He also knows I love you and not being with you isn't part of the deal. He'll just have to get over his feelings or whatever is the problem, but I think he's okay with everything."

"Shall we get this over with then?" he asked, getting to his feet and dragging her up with him.

"I guess."

He kissed her quickly on the lips. "It'll be okay, darlin'. I love you. That's all that matters."

With heavy steps, she led Jacob back to her father's room. She wasn't sure how this meeting would progress and she wasn't ready to find out. They reached the door to his room and she hesitated.

"Paige?"

"I don't know if I can do this."

He brought her hand to his lips. "We'll face him together, baby."

A heavy sigh escaped her lips in a rush. "Okay. I can do this."

They walked through the doorway together only to find her father with his eyes closed lying in the bed.

"Daddy?"

Her father didn't move.

She walked closer, picked up his hand and stroked the back with her fingers. His eyes never flickered.

"Daddy?" Her voice trembled as she shook her father's shoulder. When she turned to look at Jacob, the concern in his eyes drove terror through her heart. "Jacob?"

"I'll get the nurse." He grabbed the door as he shouted for a nurse, his voice clear with panic.

"No, Daddy. Don't do this." She shook him harder.

A nurse came rushing through the door calling her father's name. She ran her fingers along his neck to check for a pulse. "You're going to have to move, Ms. Tyler." The nurse hit an alarm on the wall and within seconds, it seemed like a hundred people rushed through the doorway.

One nurse pushed in a cart. A doctor shoved her out of the way as another nurse pushed the bed flat. They lifted him up to stick something beneath him. The moment he was flat again, another nurse started pressing on his chest.

"Jacob?" she asked moving toward him.

"Come here, darlin'. Let them work."

"It would probably be better if you took her out in the hall. This could get messy."

Jacob nodded as he wrapped an arm around her shoulders and pressed her face against his chest.

Noise. Too much noise. The loud beeping, shouting, calling out of things she didn't understand pierced her being with terror. *He's dead. He's dead.*

They took a seat on a small couch down the hall from her father's room. "What's going to happen, Jacob?"

"I don't know, honey. We'll have to wait and see."

"He's dead, isn't he?"

"Baby, I'm not a doctor, but things don't look good. I don't know what happened so I can't guess what's going on in there."

"What'll happen if he is dead? I never got to tell him about other things going on with me. I mean he doesn't know about the motorcycle or the clothes. I told him about the bar, but we didn't really discuss who I really am."

"It's God's will. Whatever happens, it's how things are supposed to be." He ran his fingers up and down her arms.

Hot tears streaked down her face as she tried not to think about what was going on in her father's room. She didn't want to know. How would she deal with not having either parent? What would her life become without her father there to guide her?

"Don't think about it for now."

"I can't help it. What'll I do if he dies?"

"You still have me."

"I know, but how will I cope not having a parent?"

"We'll get through this together."

"Thank you for being here with me."

"I wouldn't be anywhere else."

After what seemed like hours, the nurses and doctors filed out of her father's room. One of the men walked toward her with a solemn look on his face. Her heart plummeted. *No!*

"Ms. Tyler?"

"Yes?" She stood with Jacob's help, clinging onto his arm for dear life.

"I'm sorry, but there isn't anything we could do."

"No!"

"Since he'd had a stroke this morning, we fear another one took his life. I'm so sorry."

She slowly slid to the floor as racking sobs shook her frame. Jacob picked her up like she weighed no more than a child, to cradle her in his arms.

"Where can we go?"

"Follow me. The chapel is down the hall."

Numbness enveloped her in its grasp. She felt nothing, heard nothing. She clung to Jacob's shirt with a death grip. She couldn't let go. *It isn't true. It can't be true.*

Jacob took a seat on the bench with her on his lap. The feeling of his arms around her held her together even though she felt like a piece of glass shattered into a million pieces.

"Take your time. We won't move him until she's ready."

"Thank you."

They sat that way for what seemed like hours. Jacob holding her while she cried into his shirt. The wet material clung to her cheek where she pressed it to her face. She needed his strength. He didn't say anything, just held her.

"I'm sorry. I got you all wet."

"No problem, darlin'. It'll dry in no time."

She sat up, but didn't move off his lap. "We should make arrangements. Tell the church."

"In time. There's no rush."

"I don't even know his wishes. I'm assuming he wants to be buried next to my mother."

"I expect so."

She slowly got to her feet, wobbling slightly as she stood. "I'm okay."

"Are you sure? You don't look okay. You look pale and drawn."

She saw red. "I just lost my father. What the hell do you think I'm going to look like, some fucking fashion model?"

"I know you're upset, darlin', but don't take it out on me."

"You don't understand! I killed him!"

"What? No you didn't. He probably had another stroke. The doctor said so."

"But if I hadn't told him about you and the bars, he might not have had the stroke in the first place."

He cradled her in his arms as the tears came again. "Baby, strokes aren't caused by stress. God called him home."

"I hate God! I hate this whole thing! He took my mother and now he's taken my father. I have no one!"

"You've always got me."

"Do I really or will you leave me too?"

"I'm not going anywhere, darlin'."

"How do I know that? What if you decide you don't love me or you find someone else?"

"I do love you, Paige. I'm not going to find someone else. Stop talkin' crazy."

She stepped back, her heart thumping loudly in her chest. She loved him. He looked hurt and confused. How could she do this to him? "I don't know, Jacob. I need to get things taken care of for my father. Maybe you should go."

"Go where?"

"Home. I'm sure you have work you need to get done on the ranch. I'll be okay."

"I don't want to leave you, baby." He reached for her, but she stepped out of his grasp. He dropped his arms to his side with a dejected sigh. "I'll go because you asked me to, but know this, I love you and I'm not going to stop loving you any time soon." He walked out of the chapel as she sank to her knees and cried.

Chapter Fourteen

The funeral was well attended. Everyone at the church came, even some of the new members including Jacob's family. Jacob arrived with his parents, sitting in the back of the church, but she saw him just the same. Her heart ached for him to hold her, but she sat alone in the front pew dabbing her eyes as a friend of her father's led the service. Several people got up to say a few words about how wonderful he was, how caring he was, and how thoughtful of each of his parishioners he'd been over his time at the church.

Soon afterward, they all filed out to the small cemetery at the back where they laid him to rest beside her mother. Once the service had concluded, the ladies of the church put on a small reception where they fed everyone.

Paige stood alone in the corner hoping no one would approach. She didn't want to talk to anyone. She didn't want to see anyone. She only wanted one person, but he kept his distance even though his gaze never left her. She didn't know what to do anymore. She didn't want to give him the power to hurt her or leave her like her parents had done.

She felt cold, so cold.

"Are you okay?"

She looked up into Jacob's brown eyes. A quick nod was all she could manage.

He stuffed his hands in his pockets like he was afraid to touch her and probably was. The last time he tried, she backed away from him like a frightened child, which is exactly what she felt like these days.

"Thank you for coming."

"You thought I wouldn't be here for you?"

"We didn't part on good terms a few days ago."

"I told you then and I'll tell you again. I love you. I'll always be here for you no matter what, but you'll have to come to terms with the fact that I'm never going away. Yeah, your parents are gone, darlin'. People die. It's the facts of life. I can't promise I'll die after you so you won't be alone, but I'll do my damnedest to make your life the best it can be while we have the next seventy to a hundred years together."

"I don't want to risk it."

"You'd rather be alone than risk lovin' me?"

"Yes."

"Then we have nothin' more to talk about. I guess I'll see you around."

He turned on his heels and walked away.

Paige started to shake. Her whole body vibrated as she ran her hands over her arms trying to calm the chills racing through her. Her teeth even clicked together.

"Are you all right, dear?" Mrs. Johnson asked as she stopped next to her. "You look pale."

"N-no. I need to go home." Black spots appeared before her eyes. Dizziness engulfed her. She slumped against the wall to try to catch her breath, but darkness pulled at her, tempting her to give into it to escape the pain surrounding her.

The next thing she became aware of was the softness of the comforter beneath her on the bed. She didn't want to open her eyes, didn't want to face what life had thrown at her the last couple of days.

A soft voice whispered in her ear as she felt fingers stroking her face. "Paige, baby, wake up."

She slowly opened her eyes to see Jacob's concerned face hovering over her. "What happened?"

"You passed out, I'm guessin'."

"I've never fainted before in my life."

"When did you eat last?"

She glanced at the ceiling as she tried to remember.

"That's what I thought. I'm makin' you somethin' to eat. You stay right there in bed. I'll be right back." He climbed to his feet. "Don't move a muscle."

"Yes, sir."

He actually smiled at that.

A little while later, he returned with a sandwich on a plate and some chips along with a cold glass of milk. "You can't go without eating, Paige. I know you've been under a lot of stress, but it's not good for you."

"I know. It's just been so busy with arranging things for my father and such." She sat up higher in the bed before he placed the plate on her lap. "Thank you for doing this."

"No problem. How are you feeling now?"

"Better. I got dizzy before."

"I'll stay until you feel better."

"I'm fine, Jacob. You can go. I'm sure it was from not eating."

He shoved his hands in his pocket like he was afraid to touch her. Did she want him to? Yes and no. If he did, they'd end up in her bed all meshed in a tangle of arms and legs. If he didn't, he'd walk out of her life again. Right now, she needed him to leave before she threw herself at him and begged him to make love to her.

"I'll go then. You have my number. Call me if you need anything."

"I thought you didn't want to see me again?"

"I can't stop caring in a few days time, Paige. I still care a great deal. When I saw you sliding down the wall in a heap, my heart dropped into my stomach. I didn't know what was wrong. I scooped you up and brought you here."

"Why did your family attend the service? I didn't expect to see you."

"I respected your father and what he stood for. He was a good man. We came to pay our respects like any good Christian would do."

She glanced down at her toes. He'd taken her shoes off so the only thing she could focus on was the pink painted toenails on each foot. He hadn't come for her. She should have known. He wasn't happy when they parted the other day. She couldn't blame him. Pushing him out of her life because of her guilt over her father's death seemed trivial now, but she didn't know what to do. So many things needed to be taken care of. She would have to find a place to live. The church wouldn't allow her to stay in the home they'd lived in for fifteen years if her father wasn't their preacher anymore. The house would have to be cleaned out soon.

He shifted from foot to foot.

"Thank you."

"You're welcome."

He leaned down to gently kiss her on the forehead. The temptation to tilt her head up so she could capture his mouth overwhelmed her before she fought the urge. It would do no good at this point.

"Bye, darlin'."

"Bye, Jacob."

* * * *

Jacob stepped out into the bright sunlight of the summer day. His chest ached for the woman lying in the bed upstairs. He loved her, but she apparently didn't love him enough to try to make a go of this relationship they'd started. Walking away wasn't really an option. Did he have a choice? She didn't want him. It was something he had to face even though it came with difficulty. He'd never been in a position like this before. He knew he'd never loved Veronica. Even though she'd been pregnant with his child, he would have married her to give his child a father and a mother.

His father came around the corner of the church followed by the dog who had friended Paige. "Is everything all right, Jacob? I saw you carry Paige out the door."

"Yeah. I think so anyway. She passed out. I carried her back here. She's awake and eating a sandwich."

"What happened?"

"I think it's because she hasn't eaten in a couple of days. Probably several, but she couldn't remember exactly. Stubborn woman."

James smiled. "She sounds a lot like your mother."

"She is a lot like Ma. That's probably why I love her so much."

"So why are you down here and not up there with her?"

"She's got something going on in her pretty head I'm not sure how to deal with. Guilt is a hard war to wage and she's got it twofold."

"Why is that?"

"She told her father about us right before he died. She's thinking his stroke is her fault because of the stress. I can't convince her otherwise."

"Maybe talking with his doctor would help."

"There's an idea." They started walking back toward the church. The square walking stones guiding their way were worn with use. Flowers bloomed on either side of the path and he wondered absently if Paige took care of them. Gardening seemed like something she would do. Jacob paused, bringing his father to an expectant halt as well. "I'm not sure what to do about her. I love her, Dad, but she's pulling away from me."

"Give her time, son. Time heals wounds no matter how deep. She's lost both parents. It has to be difficult for her."

"But I want to help her. I want to hold her and love her."

"I know you do, Jacob. She seems like she needs the space more than you at the moment."

"How can that be? I need her, but she doesn't need me?"

"She does. She's just so torn right now, she's not sure which way to turn."

"She keeps saying she doesn't want to risk lovin' me and losin' me."

"Give her time."

Jacob sighed as he tipped his head back on his shoulders. "I guess I don't have a choice, do I?"

"Not really."

He walked back with his dad to claim their family so they could head for home. The sun slowly slipped into the afternoon sky, signaling the end of another day. Work beckoned on the ranch. It was never ending even when someone died, someone got married, a child was born, or whatever. Ranch work continued to be the one thing he always had to do even when he didn't want to. Maybe a few chores would take his mind off Paige.

The moment they hit the road to the ranch, his thoughts shifted to what needed to be done. He had more hay to stack and he'd promised Joey he would help break a couple of horses today. There would still be a few hours of daylight left before they'd call it a day.

"Where'd those two new geldings come from?"

"The Circle M."

"How is Jessica?"

Joey blushed. "I wouldn't know. I haven't seen her."

"Then why the hell are you turning red?" Jacob laughed. Joey had liked the youngest Marshall girl for some time, but he'd never made a move on her.

"It's nothin'."

"Nothin' *huh*?"

"She's too young for me anyway. She's only seventeen."

"She won't be some day."

"Don't worry about my love life. You need to figure out what's goin' on with yours."

"I wish I knew, brother. I wish I knew."

"What's goin' on now? I thought you and Paige had worked things out?"

"So did I last week, but this week things have changed again."

"Fickle woman."

Jacob laughed. "A little, yeah."

They pulled up to Jacob's parking spot before they both jumped out.

"You still want to help me break one this afternoon?" Joey asked, coming around the back of the truck.

"Sure. I could use a good kick or two. Maybe one to my head would help."

"I'll meet you back here in ten. I need to change out of these clothes." Joey laughed as he clapped Jacob on the back.

"Sure."

When they met up again a few minutes later, they headed to the barn to get the horse they would break. The palomino gelding stood in the stall happily munching on some hay.

"Come on boy. It's your turn." After grabbing the halter hanging on the nail next to the stall, Jacob slipped it over the gelding's face, hooking it behind his ears. Joey had been working with this particular horse for a bit so he wasn't too terribly gun-shy around equipment. "You've done good with him so far. He's not scared of the halter."

"I got him halter broke last week as well as blanket broke. I got the saddle on him once and he did well with it too. I think he'd ready to be ridden."

"Let's see what he's got then."

"I'll saddle Buster and get him in the round pen if you want to saddle him."

He led the horse out of the stall to the tie down area so he could get the blanket, saddle, and bridle on him without fighting with the animal since he didn't know how he would react. He trusted his brother's judgment, but it never hurt to be cautious around horses when they worked with them. The horse never baulked at the tack. Good. He'd rather save the bucking and kicking for the round pen.

Joey sat ready for him inside the pen when he came out of the barn. "You sure you want to ride him or do you want me to?"

"I'll do it. I need the rush."

Once the gate was closed behind him, he stuck his foot into the stirrup and pulled himself into the saddle. The horse didn't move for several seconds and then all hell broke loose.

The horse went straight up in a four-legged jump meant to jar the rider from his back. It did. Jacob ended up in a heap.

"Well, hell. That's a good start."

Joey laughed as he leaned over the pommel of his own saddle, resting his forearm on the leather knob.

Jacob dusted himself off as he headed for where the horse stood quivering. "Shall we go again, boy?"

The horse snorted as if to say, "Bring it on, cowboy."

Again, the horse went straight up. Jacob held on this time, gently digging his boot heels into the side of the gelding to urge him forward as Joey rode beside him. The horse dropped his head to jump again, but Jacob pulled his head up to prevent the buck. Round and round they went. The horse would throw him off, Jacob would crawl back into the saddle and they would go again.

After two hours, they finally got the horse gentled. He walked the pen circle with the pressure of Jacob's boots in his side while Joey guided the animal with a light tap of a crop to his butt.

"You've done well with him. Thanks for the help."

"No problem, brother. Anytime." As Jacob swung his leg down to dismount, the horse reared. His boot heel caught in the stirrup. Before Joey could calm the horse, Jacob had taken a hoof to the side of his chest and arm. "Fuck!"

Joey got the horse to stop by grabbing the bridle.

Jacob pulled his foot out as he rolled onto his side, grabbing his arm with his hand. "Son of a bitch!"

"You okay?"

"No. I think he broke my arm and a couple of ribs."

Joey let out a shrill whistle they saved to alert the family there'd been an accident. Within minutes, the entire family surrounded the round pen as his father moved inside to help him. "Where are you hurt?"

"My arm and ribs, I think."

"Let's get you to the hospital."

Jacob nodded. *Just fucking great. This is not what I needed.*

His father guided him out of the pen and they headed for the main lodge. A crowd of guests watched from the sidelines, whispering about riding those crazy animals. Those crazy animals are part of the ranch experience for the guests, but being hurt by one came with the job.

"Let's get this splinted so you can get off to the hospital to get some x-rays."

"Yeah. Hurts like a bitch."

Several hours later, he eased his broken body down on the bed in his trailer. The horse had broken his forearm and a couple of ribs when it had kicked him. They'd given him pain medication at the hospital. Grogginess crept into his consciousness, assisting him down into a restless sleep.

* * * *

Two bloody months. Paige hadn't talked to Jacob in two months and it was driving her batshit crazy. She'd moved herself into a small apartment, gave away most of her father's things and started her lonely life on her own. He hadn't called either, but she knew he was waiting for her to come to terms with everything going on and decide whether she wanted to risk loving him or not. She didn't know anymore. Every waking moment revolved around her memories of the time with him. Did she do the right thing? Her heart argued no, her head argued yes. She patted the dog she'd come to love on the head as he sat next to her on the floor.

Her stomach rolled. She'd had this damned flu for a week solid and it didn't seem like it was letting up anytime soon. She awoke every morning with a sour stomach and headache, threw up nothing but stomach acid, ate some toast and went back to bed. The afternoons were fine, although some days she had the icky stomach if she didn't eat something. An ulcer maybe? Who knew. With all the stress she'd been under, it wouldn't surprise her if she did have one.

Maybe it was time to see a doctor? Yeah, probably. Nothing seemed to help. Fatigue ruled her life these days. She always seemed tired and cranky.

She picked up her cell phone to dial her family doctor. *Better get this over with.*

"Doctor Orlio's office. Can I help you?"

"Yes. I need to make an appointment for a routine visit."

"Is there a specific problem you need to see the doctor for?"

"Well, I've been sick with the flu or something for a week now."

"The flu is going around even though it's an odd time of the year for it. We had a cancellation this afternoon if you'd like to come in."

"Fantastic. What time?"

She wrote down the time for her appointment and hung up the phone. Hopefully he would be able to give her some answers quickly so she could get past this and move on with her life.

By three o'clock, she sat in stunned silence in the exam room of the doctor's office. "Pregnant? You can't be serious?"

"I take it this wasn't a planned pregnancy."

"Hell, I mean, heck no! I can't be pregnant. I'm on the pill and I haven't had sex with anyone for two months!"

"Did you miss any doses about that time?"

She glanced down at her hands on her lap. *Shit.* "Yes. I missed three days. My father had a stroke and then died."

"I remember. I was sorry to hear about his death."

"Thank you, but anyway, yes I did miss some."

"There you go then."

A heavy sigh escaped her lips as tears gathered in her eyes. *What the hell is Jacob going to say?*

"Here is a prescription for some prenatal vitamins. I'll need to see you back here in one month for a checkup. You can get dressed now. I'll see you in a month."

"Thank you, doctor."

He patted her hand. "Things will work out, Paige. I'm sure you'll do what needs to be done."

"Can you tell me about abortion?"

"Is that what you're contemplating?"

Her whole body shook from the shock of this new development. *I can't raise a baby alone.* "I don't know at this point in time. I'm not sure what the father is going to think about this. We aren't together anymore and I don't know if I can raise a baby on my own."

"The nurses have some information at the desk. I'll have one of them bring it in here for you, but please don't make any hasty decisions. This isn't a simple thing to decide."

"I know. Thank you."

Several minutes later, she stood dressed and ready to leave when the nurse came in with some pamphlets. "Here is the information you requested."

"Thank you."

"I hope you aren't really thinking abortion is the way to go."

"I don't know. This whole thing is a major shock for me. It wasn't planned."

"As someone who went through this about two years ago with one of the nicest guys in the area, don't do it. I wish I hadn't."

Paige glanced at the nurse's name tag. *Veronica. Hmm.* "Thank you for the advice. I'll take that into consideration."

"You're welcome. I hope to see you in a month."

Paige left the doctor's office in a fog. Pregnant. *Now what am I going to do?* "First things first, I need to tell Jacob. It's his child too."

She glanced at the phone in her hand. Call him? No, this is something she needed to tell him in person. Something they needed to decide together.

She drove back to her apartment to get something to eat. The doctor's orders were to try to eat small meals to curb the empty stomach. She didn't think she could, but right now she felt utterly starved. After she made herself some soup, she sat down on her couch and stared at the black television screen. A baby. She touched her palm to her still flat abdomen. Jacob's baby.

"He's going to be furious." She patted the dog on the head as he pressed himself against her leg. The mutt had adopted her when she moved from the church's house to her apartment and she was lucky to have his companionship these days.

Eyes burning from unshed tears, she let them fall as she sat back against the couch. Another symptom, the doctor said. Great. She hated crying, but right now it seemed the thing to do. "Daddy?" She glanced up. "God, I wish you and Momma were here. You would know what to do."

He would never let me have an abortion. She wiped her tears with the back of her hand, attempting to fortify herself with a deep breath.

After she finished her lukewarm soup, she grabbed her jacket and keys to head to the cemetery. The drive gave her time to think about how she planned to tell Jacob about the baby. Should she just blurt it out, tell him slowly or maybe wait? The pregnancy was still in the early stages so she had time.

Luckily, the sun wouldn't set for awhile so she would have time to be able to sit and talk out her situation while she visited her parents.

She parked next to the church in the spot she used to call her own. The church parking lot was deserted today, thank goodness. The small cemetery looked forlorn in the afternoon light as the sun began its decent into the evening sky.

With a deep breath, she pushed open the door to her car so she could make her way to the spot near the back of this field of stone. Gravel crunched under her tennis shoes as she walked closer and closer to her destination. A huge oak tree shaded the area she sought. The wind picked up with a slight breeze, blowing her hair across her cheek in a caress.

"Momma?" she whispered to the wind without an answer. She rubbed both her arms to calm the chills suddenly springing up. It almost felt as if her parents were there with her.

She sank down on the soft, green grass between the headstones bearing her parent's names. A tear rolled down her cheek. "I miss you. Both of you."

The breeze picked up, rustling the few leaves on the ground.

"Help me." She wasn't sure if she was asking for God's help or her parents', but she needed someone to tell her what to do. "Tell me what I should do about this baby? I can't raise it on my own, but I don't think Jacob wants me anymore. I'm so scared."

The brush of something across her forehead calmed her heart as she heard the whispered words, "Tell him."

"What if he turns his back on me?"

"He loves you," came the reply in her daddy's voice. Should she believe her father wanted her and Jacob to be together?

She brushed some dry grass from the headstone with her mother's name. "Momma, I wish you were here to hold me. I need you so much right now."

"I love you, baby," reached her ear on the breeze. She felt as if her parents held her in a three way hug, assuring her everything would be okay.

She just had to talk to Jacob.

Chapter Fifteen

She pulled up to Jacob's trailer behind his truck and sighed. This wouldn't be easy. He would probably be angry. After all, they hadn't planned this at all. They weren't even dating anymore and here she turns up pregnant.

Her car door was whipped open, startling her into a yelp.

"What are you doin' here, Paige?" Jacob asked, holding the door open as she slipped out.

"I needed to talk to you."

He slammed the door shut behind her. "About what?"

"Can we go inside? It's kind of warm out here." Sweat trickled down between her shoulder blades. "I'm not feeling so hot."

"Sure." He led the way to his trailer, opened the door for her and then stepped back, allowing her to enter in front of him.

The cooler interior of the trailer felt like heaven on her overheated skin. She moved inside to take a seat on the couch. He took the chair opposite her. Great. He didn't even want to sit by her anymore. This wasn't going to be easy.

"Are you okay? You look pale."

"I'm okay. It's just warm."

"I didn't think it was that warm."

"Can I lie down for a minute? I don't feel so good."

"Sure. Leave your purse there and you can lie down on my bed. I'll get you a cool rag for your forehead. Are you sick?"

"A little. I've been sick for about a week. This is the first day I've really been out of the house for any length of time."

"Well whatever we have to talk about could have waited until you felt better," he said, holding her arm as they walked down the hall to his bedroom. Once he had her on the bed, he retrieved a cool cloth from the bathroom and draped it over her eyes. "Better?"

"I've got a splitting headache. Could you grab the Tylenol out of my purse? I should take a couple."

"Of course."

When he didn't come back for several minutes, she began to wonder what the hell was taking him so long. He should have been able to find the Tylenol in her purse easy enough. "Jacob?" she called, removing the washcloth and sitting up only to find him standing in the doorway of his bedroom holding the pamphlets on abortion in his hands.

"You're pregnant?"

"I, *uh…*"

"Answer me!"

"Apparently, yes. I went to the doctor today. I thought it was the flu."

He waved the pamphlets in front of her face. "No abortion, Paige. Don't even think about it. I won't let you."

"But Jacob—"

He began pacing back and forth next to the bed, clenching his fists. "No. I went through this once before and I'm not going through it again. This is the reason I kept drinking myself into a stupor."

"Over someone being pregnant?"

"Yes. I got a girl in town pregnant. We talked about abortion because she didn't want the baby, but I begged her not to. She did it anyway and told me two days later. The guilt drove me to drink. My child would have been born by now."

"God, Jacob. I'm sorry. I didn't know."

He raked his fingers through his hair, dislodging his cowboy hat behind him. "You can't abort it, Paige. Please."

"I wanted us to talk about this. It wasn't planned. Hell, I was on birth control, but I missed a couple of days right around the time we were together last."

"I don't want to talk about it. I love you. I haven't stopped loving you and I'll love a baby we made together no matter what the circumstances." He pulled her to her feet and wrapped his arms around her as he buried his face in her hair. "Baby, please don't abort my child."

"I won't, Jacob. I promise, I won't."

He pushed her back, cupped her face between his hands and said, "Marry me."

"What?"

"Marry me, right now. Today. Whenever. I don't care. I want us to be a family." His eyes brimmed with tears. "I love you."

"Are you serious?"

"Yes I'm serious. What do I have to do to prove it to you? I've been miserable the last two months. Do you have any idea how many times I've picked up the phone to call you before putting it back down?" He placed a small peck of a kiss to her lips before he continued, “A million times, that’s how many, but I knew you needed time to get past your doubts.”

Tears rolled down her cheeks and he brushed them away with his thumbs. *Damn hormones.* “You still love me?”

“More than anything. Say you’ll marry me, please?”

“Yes. Yes, I’ll marry you.”

“What about all the guilt you’ve been feeling?”

“I sat down and had a long talk with both my parents at the cemetery this afternoon when I returned from the doctor’s office and I realized it wasn’t my fault they died. Both instances were controlled by someone much higher than I am. I just hope I can adopt your family. Do you think there is room for one more?”

“Oh, hell yeah! My mom already loves you and I’m sure my dad will become like a second father to you. They’ll spoil any baby we have together like they spoil their other grandchildren.”

“Terri had her baby?”

“Yeah, another little boy. They have two now.”

He leaned in, taking her lips in a panty melting kiss obviously meant to break any resistance she might have had to keeping his baby or marrying him. Not that she planned to resist either situation. She loved him and wanted to be with him always.

As their kiss ended, she stepped back. “I want a wedding.”

“Okay.” He stepped toward her.

“We can plan something quick. At my father’s church.” She stepped back again.

He moved forward. “Anything you want, baby.”

"A ring."

"We'll go buy one right now. I have money saved up. It might not be huge, but you can pick what you want."

"I don't want a huge ring, Jacob. Whatever you think is appropriate, I'll love." Her knees hit the bed. "Can we make love now?"

"I thought you'd never ask, but I thought you had a headache?"

"I feel a hundred percent better knowing you love me and want this baby."

"More than anything in this world."

"How do you feel about a dog?"

"Dog?"

"The big yellow one. He's part of the bargain."

"I love animals so I don't see why we couldn't use another protective member of the family around here."

Epilogue

Moonlight caressed her skin through the gauzy curtains of the cabana. Jacob slowly slid his fingers from the curve of her hip to the edge of her breast as she sifted the hair on his chest through her fingertips.

"I love you."

"I love you too."

"I wish we could stay like this forever, but unfortunately, we have to go home tomorrow."

"I know," she whispered, her lips caressing his chest.

His cock hardened even though they'd just finished making love. *God, I'm insatiable around her*. Good thing she'd married him a week ago.

The wedding was a small, intimate affair at her father's church with the preacher who'd done her father's eulogy performing the ceremony. Only the church members, her friends from the pre-school and a few dozen family and friends of the Young's were in attendance. It still filled up the little church with the white steeple.

Paige had worn her mother's wedding dress. She looked like a princess in the stark white gown with the beautifully beaded bodice and skirt.

His father had walked her down the aisle after Paige had insisted she needed him to be her fill-in father. They had a great little discussion just the two of them about a father's love. A discussion he wasn't privy to except to know they'd talked. His father had tears in his eyes when he'd handed her over to Jacob at the altar. Jacob knew there would be bond between his wife and his father, from that day forward, no man would ever break and he loved his father even more for becoming that for her.

"What are you thinking about?"

"Our wedding."

"Why?"

"You were beautiful."

"Thank you, but you cut a pretty handsome cowboy in your tux jacket, black jeans and boots. I loved the black Stetson too. Wow."

"Should I fuck you with just my hat on?"

"Would you?"

He roared with laughter. "Anything you want, darlin'."

She crawled on top of him, straddling his hips. "I want you. Like this. Right now."

His cock was at full attention. "I could go for that."

She eased her pussy down his cock a slow inch at a time until he was fully inside her. "God, I love how you feel inside me."

"I love how you surround me with your heat. Ride me, baby."

She lifted her body until only the head of his cock still rested inside her. She made several shallow dips that had him panting his need.

"You're teasing me."

"*Uh-huh.*"

"Wench." He quickly rolled her over onto her back, pushed her legs up until the bend of her knee rested over his forearms and shoved his cock inside her. The heat of her pussy was his undoing. He couldn't keep himself from pushing so deep that she growled low in response. He loved when she did that.

"Please, Jacob."

"Please wait, babe?"

"Oh God, no. Don't wait. Fuck me just like that."

"Your wish is my command." He fucked her so hard she had to brace herself against the headboard. Luckily they were in a small independent cabana where they had no neighbors. They had been kind of loud in their love making over the week they'd been there. If she wasn't already pregnant, he surely would have made her that way this week.

He felt her pussy quiver around his cock. With his thumb against her clit, he drove her into a screaming orgasm as she cried his name out in between panting breaths.

He slowed his thrusts.

"No, God, don't stop. Please."

"More."

"Hell yes. More."

He pulled out much to her whimpers of need, flipped her over so she was on her hands and knees and shoved back inside.

"Yes, yes."

"I don't want to hurt you or the baby."

"You won't. Please, Jacob. God, please."

He reached around to pinch her nipple between his thumb and finger, knowing the pain would send her over the edge again.

"Oh yes."

The sucking sounds their bodies made as he fucked her drove his desire to screaming proportions. He knew he wouldn't last much longer, but he wanted to make her come one more time. "Do you have another one in there for me?"

"I don't think I can."

"Sure you can," he said, dragging his finger through the wetness between her legs to clasp her clit in a heavy pinch.

She exploded again, coating his cock in cum and bringing him to a moaning, thrashing of the hips orgasm and probably killing off a few brain cells in the mix.

His body shook from the force of his release as he eased down beside her and drew her against his side. "You are magnificent."

"You're pretty good yourself there, handsome."

They lay side by side quietly for several minutes before he spoke again. "What do you want the baby to be, a boy or a girl?"

"I don't really care as long as it's healthy."

"You know what I want?"

"What?"

"A beautiful little girl who looks like her mother."

"You're gonna make me cry."

"No crying."

She swiped at the tears rolling down her cheeks. "You know I can't help it, Jacob. I'm such a mess these days with this pregnancy."

He laid his hand on her slightly rounded belly. "Baby, I love you more every day and if that means putting up with a few tears, then so be it."

"I love you with all my heart. I hope you're happy."

"I'm ecstatic! I can't believe how great my life as turned out. I have a beautiful wife, a new baby on the way, a good job, we're working on building our own house on my piece of land, and my investments guided by my brother Jeremiah, are turning into real moneymakers. Who could ask for more?"

"*Um*, Jacob?"

"Yeah, baby."

"How would you feel about twins?

The End

About the Author

Sandy Sullivan is a romance author, who, when not writing, spends her time with her husband Shaun on their farm in middle Tennessee. She loves to ride her horses, play with their dogs and relax on the porch, enjoying the rolling hills of her home south of Nashville. Country music is a passion of hers and she loves to listen to it while she writes.

She is an avid reader of romance novels and enjoys reading Nora Roberts, Jude Deveraux and Susan Wiggs. Finding new authors and delving into something different helps feed the need for literature. A registered nurse by education, she loves to help people and spread the enjoyment of romance to those around her with her novels. She loves cowboys so you'll find many of her novels have sexy men in tight jeans and cowboy boots.

Other Books by Sandy

Love Me Once, Love Me Twice (Montana Cowboys 1)
Before the Night is Over (Montana Cowboys 2)
Two for the Price of One (Montana Cowboys 3)
Difficult Choices (Montana Cowboys 4)
Doctor Me Up (Montana Cowboys 5)
Gotta Love a Cowboy
Country Minded Cougar
Taming the Cougar
Meet Me in the Barn
Trouble with a Cowboy

Stakin' His Claim (Behind the Chutes 2)
Forever Kind of Love (Five Hearts Anthology)
Love After All (The Call of Duty Anthology)
Make Mine a Cowboy (Cowboy Dreamin' 1)
Healing a Cowboy's Heart (Cowboy Dreamin' 2)

Secret Cravings Publishing
www.secretcravingspublishing.com

Made in the USA
Charleston, SC
05 March 2014